Reader's Digest

BEST LOVED BOOKS
FOR YOUNG READERS

The Call of the Wild

A CONDENSATION OF THE BOOK BY

Jack London

Illustrated by John Schoenherr

and

Typhoon

A CONDENSATION OF THE BOOK BY

Joseph Conrad

Illustrated by Frank Mullins

CHOICE PUBLISHING, INC.

New York

PRODUCED IN ASSOCIATION WITH MEDIA PROJECTS INCORPORATED

Executive Editor, Carter Smith
Managing Editor, Jeanette Mall
Project Editor, Jacqueline Ogburn
Associate Editor, Charles Wills
Art Director, Bernard Schleifer

Library of Congress Catalog Number: 88-63348
ISBN: 0-945260-28-8

This 1989 edition is published and distributed by Choice Publishing, Inc.,
Great Neck, NY 11021, with permission of The Reader's Digest Association, Inc.

Manufactured in the United States of America.

10 9 8 7 6 5 4 3 2

Contents

Foreword

DURING THE KLONDIKE gold rush, sled dogs were in great demand to carry adventurous men and precious metals across the frozen wastes. Many a handsome and gentle dog was stolen from his rightful master in the United States and shipped north to be pressed into that hard service. There in the wilderness, where only the law of club and fang prevailed, none but the strongest, most courageous animals survived.

Buck, the hero of *The Call of the Wild,* was such a dog. And Jack London, who has made Buck one of the most famous animals in all fiction, knew many of his kind. London was only twenty-one when reports of a fortune to be had for the taking lured him to Alaska. He failed to strike it rich in the goldfields, but out of his experiences came this thrilling novel, which at once established his success as a writer.

Born near San Francisco in 1876, Jack knew from childhood what it means to live by one's courage and wits. He quit school early to work as an "oyster pirate," robbing the nets of other fishermen and selling their catch in the market. For a while he was a sailor on board a seal-hunting schooner. Later he studied for a year at the University of California. But his real education came from his roving life as a seaman, a longshoreman, a war correspondent (in the Russo-Japanese War), and a gold hunter in the Klondike.

Jack London became the most popular and highly paid writer of his day, but he never forgot his own struggle to make his way in life. His books are filled with feats of bravery and resourcefulness in the face of constant danger, and with the harsh beauty of wild nature.

In just sixteen years Jack London produced fifty books, including *The Sea-Wolf, White Fang, Martin Eden,* and *The Mutiny of the Elsinore*—all of them immensely popular. But he spent his money as fast as he made it. He lived so hard he ruined his health, and he died at the age of forty.

THE
CALL OF THE
WILD

BUCK DID NOT READ the newspapers, or he would have known that trouble was brewing, not alone for himself, but for every tidewater dog, strong of muscle and with warm, long hair, from Puget Sound to San Diego. For men, groping in the Arctic darkness, had found a yellow metal; and steamship companies had boomed the find, and now thousands were rushing into the Northland. They all wanted dogs, and the dogs they wanted were heavy dogs, with strong muscles by which to toil, and furry coats to protect them from the frost.

Buck lived at Judge Miller's place in the sun-kissed Santa Clara Valley. The big house, half hidden by tall poplars through which glimpses could be caught of the wide, cool veranda that surrounded it, was approached by driveways winding through wide-spreading lawns. At the rear, there were great stables where a dozen grooms and boys held forth, rows of vine-clad servants' cottages, a big swimming pool, and then long grape arbors, green pastures, orchards and berry patches.

Over this great demesne Buck ruled. Here he was born, and here he had lived the four years of his life. His father, Elmo, a huge St. Bernard, had been the Judge's inseparable companion. Buck was not so large, for his mother, Shep, had been a Scotch shepherd dog. Nevertheless, his one hundred and forty pounds, to which was added the dignity that comes of good living and universal respect, enabled him to carry himself in right royal fashion. He escorted the Judge's daughters on long rambles, carried the Judge's grandsons on his back and, on wintry nights, lay at the Judge's feet before the roaring library fire. He had a fine pride in himself and was even a trifle egotistical, as country gentlemen sometimes become. But hunting, plunging in the swimming pool and kindred delights with the Judge's sons had hardened his muscles, and saved him from being a mere pampered house dog.

This was the manner of dog Buck was in the fall of 1897, when the Klondike gold strike dragged men from all the world into the frozen North. But Buck did not read the newspapers, and he did not know that Manuel, one of the gardener's helpers, was an undesirable acquaintance. Manuel had one besetting sin—he was a gambler; and he had one besetting weakness—faith in a system, and this made his damnation certain. For to play a system requires money, while the wages of a gardener's helper do not lap over the needs of a wife and numerous progeny.

The Judge was at a meeting on the memorable night of Manuel's treachery. No one saw him and Buck go off through the orchard on what Buck imagined was merely a stroll. And only one man saw them arrive at the little flag station known as College Park. This man talked with Manuel, and money chinked between them.

"You might wrap up the goods before you deliver 'em," the stranger said gruffly, and Manuel doubled a piece of stout rope around Buck's neck under the collar.

"Twist it, an' you'll choke 'em plentee," said Manuel.

Buck had accepted the rope with quiet dignity. To be sure, it was an unwonted performance: but he had learned to trust in men he knew, and to give them credit for a wisdom that outreached his own. But when the ends of the rope were placed in the stranger's hands, he growled menacingly, in his pride believing that merely to intimate was to command. But to his surprise the rope tightened around his neck, shutting off his breath. In quick rage he sprang at the man, who met him halfway, grappled him close by the throat and with a deft twist threw him over on his back. Then the rope tightened mercilessly while Buck struggled in a fury, his tongue lolling out of his mouth and his great chest panting. Never in all his life had he been so vilely treated, and never had he been so angry. But his strength ebbed, his eyes glazed, and he could do nothing when the two men put him into a crate. Then the train was flagged and they threw him into the baggage car.

For two nights and days, imprisoned in his crate, Buck neither ate nor drank. High-strung and feverish, he accumulated a fund of wrath that boded ill for whoever first fell foul of him. His eyes turned bloodshot, and he was metamorphosed into a raging fiend. The Judge would not have recognized him; and the expressmen breathed with relief when they bundled him off the train at Seattle.

Four men gingerly carried the crate from the wagon into a small high-walled backyard. A stout man, with a red sweater that sagged at the neck, signed the book for the driver. That, Buck divined, was the next tormentor, and he hurled himself savagely against the bars. The man smiled grimly and drove a hatchet into the crate to make an opening sufficient for the passage of Buck's body.

"Now, you red-eyed devil," he said, dropping the hatchet and picking up a club.

And Buck truly looked like a red-eyed devil as he drew himself together for the spring, hair bristling, mouth foaming, a mad glitter in his bloodshot eyes. Straight at the man he launched his one hundred and forty pounds of surcharged fury. In midair, just as his jaws were about to close on the man, he received a shock that checked his body and brought his teeth together with an agonizing clip. He whirled over, fetching the ground on his back and side. He had never been struck by a club in his life, and did not understand. With a snarl that was part bark and more scream he sprang again. And again the shock brought him crushingly to the ground. This time he was aware that it was the club, but his madness knew no caution. A dozen times he charged, and as often the club smashed him down.

3

After a particularly fierce blow, he crawled to his feet, too dazed to rush. He staggered limply about, blood flowing from nose and mouth and ears, his beautiful coat sprayed and flecked with it. Then the man advanced and deliberately dealt him a frightful blow on the nose. All the pain he had endured was as nothing compared with the exquisite agony of this. With a roar he again hurled himself at the man. But the man struck the shrewd blow he had purposely withheld for so long, and Buck described a complete circle in the air, then crashed senseless to the ground.

When his senses came back, his strength did not. He lay where he had fallen, and watched the man in the red sweater.

"Well, Buck, my boy," the man said, "you've learned your place, and I know mine. Be a good dog and all'll go well; be a bad dog, and I'll whale the stuffin' outa you. Understand?"

As he spoke he fearlessly patted the head he had so mercilessly pounded, and though Buck's hair involuntarily bristled at the touch, he endured it without protest. When the man brought him water he drank eagerly, and later bolted a generous meal of raw meat, chunk by chunk, from the man's hand.

He was beaten (he knew that); but he was not broken. He saw, once for all, that he stood no chance against a man with a club. He had learned a lesson, and he never forgot it. That club was his introduction to the reign of primitive law, and he met the introduction halfway. Life took on a fiercer aspect, and he faced it with all the latent cunning of his nature aroused.

As the days went by, he watched other dogs pass under the dominion of the man in the red sweater. Again and again the lesson was driven home: a man with a club was a lawgiver to be obeyed, not necessarily conciliated. Of this last Buck was never guilty, though he did see beaten dogs that fawned upon the man, and wagged their tails, and licked his hand. And he saw one dog, that would neither conciliate nor obey, finally killed in the struggle for mastery.

Now and again strangers came, gave money to the man in the red sweater, and took one or more dogs away.

4

One day there was a little wizened man who looked at Buck and cried: "*Sacrédam!* Dat one dam' bully dog! Eh? How moch?"

"Three hundred, and a present at that," was the prompt reply. "And seein' it's government money, you ain't got no kick coming, eh, Perrault?"

Perrault grinned. Considering that the price of dogs was booming, it was not an unfair sum for so fine an animal. As courier for the Canadian Government, bearing important dispatches, he was anxious to secure the best dogs. When he looked at Buck he commented mentally that he was "one in ten t'ousand."

So, along with Curly, a good-natured Newfoundland, Buck was led away by the little wizened man. That was the last he saw of the man in the red sweater, and as Curly and he looked at receding Seattle from the deck of the *Narwhal*, it was the last he saw of the warm Southland. Perrault took the dogs below and turned them over to a black-faced giant called François. Perrault was a French Canadian and swarthy; but François was a French-Canadian half-breed, and twice as swarthy. They were a new kind of men to Buck, and he grew to respect them. They were fair, impartial in administering justice and wise in the way of dogs.

In the tween decks of the *Narwhal*, Buck and Curly joined two other dogs. One of them was a big, snow-white fellow from Spitzbergen. He was friendly, in a treacherous sort of way, smiling while he meditated some underhand trick, as, for instance, when he stole from Buck's food at the first meal. As Buck sprang to punish him, the lash of François's whip sang through the air, reaching the culprit first; and nothing remained to Buck but to recover the bone.

The other dog was a gloomy, morose fellow. He showed plainly that all he desired was to be left alone, and that there would be trouble if he were not. "Dave" he was called, and he ate and slept, and took interest in nothing, not even when the *Narwhal* rolled and bucked like a thing possessed. When Buck and Curly grew excited, half wild with fear, he raised his head, favored them with an incurious glance, yawned, and went to sleep again.

At last, one morning, the ship's propeller stopped throbbing and the *Narwhal* was pervaded with excitement. François leashed the dogs and brought them on deck. At the first step upon the cold surface, Buck's feet sank into a white mushy something that felt very like mud. He sprang back with a snort. More of this white stuff was falling through the air. He shook himself, but more of it fell upon him. He sniffed it curiously, then licked some up on his tongue. It bit like fire, and the next instant was gone. This puzzled him. He tried it again, with the same result. The onlookers laughed uproariously, and he felt ashamed. It was his first snow.

≫ CHAPTER II ≪

BUCK'S FIRST DAY at the camp on the Dyea beach was like a nightmare. He had been jerked from the heart of civilization and flung into the heart of things primordial. Here was neither peace, nor rest, nor a moment's safety. There was imperative need to be constantly alert; for these dogs and men were not town dogs and men, and they knew no law but the savage law of club and fang.

He had never seen dogs fight as these creatures fought, and his first experience taught him another unforgettable lesson. Curly was the victim. They were camped near the log store, where she, in her friendly way, made advances to a husky the size of a full-grown wolf, though not half so large as she. There was no warning, only a leap in like a flash, a metallic clip of teeth, a swift leap out, and Curly's face was ripped open from eye to jaw.

It was the wolf manner of fighting, to strike and leap away; but there was more to it than this. Thirty or forty huskies ran to the spot and surrounded the combatants in an intent and silent circle, licking their chops. Curly rushed her antagonist, who struck again and leaped aside. He met her next rush with his chest, and tumbled her off her feet. She never regained them. This was what the onlooking huskies had waited for. They closed in upon her, snarling and yelping, and she was buried, screaming with agony, beneath the bristling mass of bodies.

So sudden was it, and so unexpected, that Buck was taken aback. He saw Spitz run out his scarlet tongue in a way he had of laughing; and he saw François, swinging an axe, spring into the mess of dogs. Three men with clubs were helping to scatter them. It did not take long. But Curly lay there limp and lifeless in the bloody, trampled snow, almost literally torn to pieces. So that was the way. Once down, that was the end of you. Spitz ran out his tongue and laughed again, and from that moment Buck hated him with a bitter and deathless hatred.

Before he had recovered from this shock he received another. François fastened upon him a harness, such as he had seen put on the horses at home. And as he had seen horses work, so he was set to work, hauling François on a sled to the forest that fringed the valley, and returning with a load of firewood. Though his dignity was hurt, he was too wise to rebel. François was stern, and by virtue of his whip received instant obedience; while Dave, who was an experienced wheeler, nipped Buck's hindquarters whenever he was in error. Spitz, the leader, also experienced, growled reproof or cunningly threw his weight in the traces to jerk Buck into the way he should go.

Buck learned easily, and by the time they returned to camp he knew enough to stop at "Ho," to go ahead at "Mush," to swing wide on the bends, and to keep clear of the wheeler when the loaded sled shot downhill at their heels.

"T'ree vair' good dogs," François told Perrault. "Dat Buck, heem pool lak hell. I tich heem queek as anyt'ing."

By afternoon, Perrault, who was in a hurry to be on the trail to Dawson with his dispatches, returned with three more dogs. Two were brothers, Billee and Joe he called them. Billee's one fault was his excessive good nature, while Joe was the very opposite, sour and introspective, with a perpetual snarl and a malignant eye. Spitz first thrashed Billee, who cried and ran away when Spitz's sharp teeth scored his flank, and then turned on Joe. But no matter how Spitz circled, Joe whirled to face him, and so terrible was his appearance that Spitz was forced to forgo disciplining him. The third was an old battle-scarred husky, with a single eye which flashed a warning of prowess. He was called Sol-leks, which means the Angry One. Like Dave, he asked nothing, gave nothing, expected nothing; and when he marched slowly and deliberately into their midst, even Spitz left him alone. His one peculiarity was that he did not like to be approached on his blind side. Of this offense Buck was unwittingly guilty, and Sol-leks whirled upon him and slashed his shoulder to the bone for three inches up and down. Forever after Buck avoided his blind side, and had no more trouble.

That night Buck faced the great problem of sleeping. The tent, illumined by a candle, glowed warmly in the snow, but when he entered it, Perrault and François bombarded him with curses and cooking utensils, till he fled ignominiously into the outer cold. A chill wind nipped him sharply and bit into his wounded shoulder. He lay down on the snow, but the frost soon drove him shivering to his feet. Miserable and disconsolate, he wandered about the tents of the great camp, only to find that one place was as cold as another. Here and there savage dogs rushed upon him, but he bristled his neck hair and snarled (he was learning fast), and they let him go his way unmolested.

His own teammates had disappeared. Where could they possibly be? With drooping tail and shivering body, he aimlessly circled Perrault's tent. Suddenly the snow gave way beneath his forelegs. Something wriggled under his feet. He sprang back, bristling, fearful of the unseen. But a friendly little yelp reassured him, and he went back to investigate. A whiff of warm air ascended to his nostrils, and there, curled up under the snow in a snug ball, lay Billee. He whined placatingly, squirmed and wriggled to show his goodwill, and even ventured to lick Buck's face with his warm, wet tongue.

So that was the way they did it. Buck selected a spot, and with much fuss and waste effort proceeded to dig a hole for himself. In a trice the heat from his body filled the confined space and he was asleep.

When roused by the noises of the waking camp, he did not know at first where he was. It had snowed during the night and he was completely buried. The white walls pressed him on every side, and fear surged through him. It was fear of the wild thing for the trap, harking back to the lives of his forebears; for he was a civilized dog, and of his own experience knew no trap. The muscles of his whole body contracted instinctively, and with a snarl he bounded straight up into the blinding day, the snow flying about him in a flashing cloud.

A shout from François hailed his appearance. "Wot I say?" he cried to Perrault. "Dat Buck sure learn queek as anyt'ing."

Inside an hour three more huskies were added to the team, making a total of nine dogs, and before another quarter of an hour had passed they were in harness and swinging up the trail toward the Dyea Canyon. Buck was glad to be gone, and the surprising eagerness which animated the whole team was communicated to him. Dave and Sol-leks were utterly transformed by the harness. All passiveness and unconcern had dropped from them. They were alert and active, anxious that the work should go well, and fiercely irritable with whatever retarded that work. The toil of the traces seemed all that they lived for and the only thing in which they took delight.

Dave was wheeler, next to the sled; pulling in front of him was Buck, then Sol-leks; the rest of the team was strung out ahead, single file, to Spitz, the leader.

Buck had been placed between Dave and Sol-leks so that he might receive instruction. Apt scholar that he was, they were equally apt teachers, never allowing him to linger long in error, and enforcing their teaching with sharp teeth. Dave was fair and very wise. He never nipped Buck without cause, and he never failed to nip him when he stood in need of it. As François's whip backed him up, Buck found it cheaper to mend his ways than to retaliate. Once, during a halt, when he got tangled in the traces and delayed the start, both Dave and Sol-leks flew at him. Thereafter, Buck took care to keep the traces clear, and long before the day was done, his mates had ceased to nag him.

It was a hard day's run, up the canyon, through Sheep Camp, past the timberline, across glaciers and snowdrifts hundreds of feet deep, and over the great Chilkoot Divide, which stands between the salt water and the fresh and guards forbiddingly the sad and lonely North.

They made good time down the chain of lakes which fills the craters of extinct volcanoes, and late that night pulled into the huge camp at the head of Lake Bennett, where thousands of gold seekers were building boats against the breakup of the ice in the spring. Buck made his hole in the snow and slept the sleep of the exhausted just, but all too early next morning was routed out and harnessed with his mates again.

That day they made forty miles on well-packed snow; but the next day, and for many days to follow, they broke their own trail, and made poorer time. As a rule, Perrault traveled ahead of the team, packing the snow with webbed shoes to make it easier for them. François, guiding the sled from the gee pole at its front sometimes exchanged places with him, but not often. Perrault was in a hurry, and his expert knowledge of ice was indispensable, for the fall ice was very thin, and where there was swift water, there was no ice at all.

Day after day, they were off at the first gray of dawn and did not pitch camp again till after dark. Buck was ravenous. The pound and a half of sun-dried salmon which was his ration never seemed enough. He suffered perpetual hunger pangs. Yet the other dogs, because they weighed less and were born to the life, received a pound only of the fish and managed to keep in good condition.

He swiftly lost his old fastidiousness. A dainty eater, he found that his mates, finishing first, robbed him of his unfinished ration. There was no defending it. While he was fighting off two or three, it disappeared down the throats of the others. So he ate as fast as they; and, compelled by hunger, he was not above taking what did not belong to him. Once he saw Pike, one of the new dogs, a clever malingerer and thief, slyly steal a slice of bacon when Perrault's back was turned. Buck duplicated the performance the following day, getting away with the whole chunk. A great uproar was raised, but he was unsuspected.

This first theft marked the decay of Buck's moral nature, a vain thing in this ruthless struggle for existence. It was all well enough in the Southland, under the law of love and fellowship, to respect private property; but in the Northland, under the law of club and fang, whoso took such things into account would fail to prosper. He did not steal for joy of it, but because of the clamor of his stomach. He did not rob openly, but secretly and cunningly, to save his hide.

His development (or retrogression) was rapid. His muscles became hard as iron and he grew callous to all ordinary pain. He could eat anything, no matter how loathsome; his sight became remarkably keen, while his hearing developed such acuteness that in his sleep he heard the faintest sound and knew what it heralded. He learned to bite the ice out with his teeth when it collected between his toes; and when he was thirsty and there was a thick scum of ice over the water hole, he would break it by rearing and striking it with stiff forelegs. He could scent the wind and forecast it so that, no matter how breathless the air when he dug his nest by tree or bank, the wind that later blew inevitably found him to leeward, sheltered and snug.

And not only did he learn by experience, but dead instincts became alive again. The domesticated generations fell from him. It was no task for him to learn to fight with the quick wolf snap, for such tricks had been stamped into the heredity of the breed by his forgotten ancestors. And when, on the still, cold nights, he pointed his nose at a star and howled, his cadences were theirs, the cadences which voiced their woe and what to them was the meaning of the stillness, and the cold, and dark.

Thus, as token of what a puppet thing life is, the ancient song surged through him and he came into his own again; and he came because men had found a yellow metal in the North, and because Manuel was a gardener's helper whose wages did not lap over the needs of his wife and divers small copies of himself.

⋙ CHAPTER III ⋘

THE DOMINANT PRIMORDIAL BEAST was strong in Buck, and under the fierce conditions of trail life it grew and grew. Yet it was a secret growth. His newborn cunning gave him poise and control. He avoided fights whenever possible. A certain deliberateness characterized his attitude: in the bitter hatred between him and Spitz he betrayed no impatience, shunned all offensive acts.

Spitz, on the other hand, went out of his way to bully Buck, striving constantly to start the fight which could end only in the death of one or the other. Early in the trip this almost took place. Driving snow and a wind that cut like a white-hot knife forced them one night to grope for a camping place on the shore of Lake Laberge. They could hardly have fared worse. At their backs rose a perpendicular wall of rock, and Perrault and François were compelled to make their driftwood fire and spread their sleeping robes on the ice of the lake itself. The tent they had left at Dyea in order to travel light. The fire soon thawed down through the ice and left them to eat supper in the dark.

Close in under the sheltering rock Buck made his nest. So snug and warm was it that he was loath to leave it when François distributed the fish. But when he had finished his ration and returned, he found his nest occupied. A warning snarl told him that the trespasser was Spitz. This was too much. He sprang upon Spitz with a fury which surprised them both. When they shot out in a tangle from the disrupted nest, François divined the cause of the trouble. "Gif it to heem, by Gar!" he cried to Buck. "Gif it to heem, the dirty t'eef!"

Spitz was crying with sheer rage and eagerness as he circled back and forth for a chance to spring in. Buck was no less eager, and no less cautious. Then the unexpected happened, and postponed their struggle.

An oath from Perrault, the resounding impact of a club upon a bony frame, and a shrill yelp of pain, heralded pandemonium. The place was suddenly alive with skulking furry forms—starving huskies who had scented the camp from some Indian village. The two men sprang among them with clubs but they fought back. They were crazed by the smell of food. Perrault found one with head buried in his and François's grub box. His club landed heavily on the gaunt ribs, and the grub box was capsized on the ground. On the instant a score of famished brutes were scrambling for bread and bacon. They yelped and howled under the rain of blows, but struggled none the less madly till the last morsel had been devoured.

In the meantime more of the invaders had set upon the astonished team dogs and had swept them back against the cliff. Never had Buck seen such dogs. They were skeletons, draped in draggled hides, with blazing eyes and slavered fangs. He was beset by three, and in a trice his head and shoulders were ripped and slashed. The din was frightful. Billee was crying as usual. Dave and Sol-leks, dripping blood from a score of wounds, were fighting bravely side by side. Joe was snapping like a demon.

At last, terrified into a kind of bravery, Billee sprang through the savage circle and fled away over the ice. Pike and the two other huskies added to the team at Dyea, Dub and Dolly, followed, with the rest of the team on their heels. As Buck drew himself together to spring after them, out of the tail of his eye he saw Spitz rush upon him with the evident intention of overthrowing him. Once off his feet and under that mass of huskies, there would be no hope for him. But he braced to the shock of Spitz's charge, then joined the flight out on the lake.

At daybreak the wounded team limped warily back to camp in a sorry plight to find the marauders gone and the two men in bad tempers. Half their grub supply was gone. The huskies had chewed through the sled lashings and canvas coverings. They had eaten a pair of Perrault's moccasins, chunks out of the leather traces, and even two feet of lash from the end of François's whip. He broke from a mournful contemplation of it to look over his grievously wounded dogs.

"Ah, my frien's," he said softly, "mebbe it mek you mad dog, dose many bites. Mebbe all mad dog, *sacrédam!* Wot you t'ink, eh, Perrault?" The courier shook his head dubiously. With four hundred miles still between him and Dawson, he could ill afford to have madness break out among his dogs. And the hardest part of the trail was just ahead.

The Thirty Mile River was wide open. Although a cold snap was on, fifty below zero, its wild water still defied the frost, and the ice held in the eddies only. Six days of exhausting toil were required to cover those thirty terrible miles, and every foot of them was accomplished at peril of life to dog and man. A dozen times, Perrault, nosing the way, broke through the ice bridges, saved by a long pole which he so held that it fell each time across the hole made by his body.

Nothing daunted him. He took all manner of risks, resolutely skirting the shores on rim ice that bent and crackled underfoot and upon which they dared not halt. Once, the sled broke through, with Dave and Buck, and they were half frozen and all but drowned by the time they were dragged out. They were coated solidly with ice, and to save them, the two men kept them on the run around a fire, sweating and thawing, so close that they were singed by the flames.

By the time they made the Hootalinqua and good ice, Buck was played out. His feet were not yet so hard as a husky's. All day he limped in agony, and camp once made, lay like a dead dog. Hungry as he was, he would not move, even for his ration of fish. So François brought it to him, and then rubbed his feet for half an hour. Then he sacrificed the tops of his own moccasins to make four moccasins for Buck. Even Perrault had to grin one morning after that, when François forgot to put them on him and Buck lay on his back, his feet waving appealingly in the air, and refused to budge without them.

One morning, Dolly went suddenly mad, giving a long, heartbreaking howl that made every dog bristle with fear; then she sprang straight for Buck. He had never seen a dog go mad; yet he knew that here was horror, and fled from it in panic. Away he raced, with Dolly, panting and frothing, one leap behind. A quarter of a mile away he heard François call and he doubled back, still one leap ahead, gasping for air, all his faith now in François. The driver's axe was poised, and as Buck shot past, he crashed it down upon mad Dolly's head.

Buck staggered over against the sled, exhausted, sobbing for breath, helpless. This was Spitz's opportunity. He sprang on Buck, and twice his teeth sank into his unresisting foe and ripped and tore the flesh to the bone. Then François's lash descended, and Buck saw Spitz receive the worst whipping as yet administered to any of the team.

"One devil, dat Spitz," remarked Perrault. "Some dam' day heem keel dat Buck."

"Dat Buck two devils," was François's rejoinder. "All de tam I watch dat Buck I know for sure. Lissen: some dam' fine day heem get mad lak hell an' den heem chew dat Spitz all up an' spit heem out on de snow. Sure. I know."

Spitz, as acknowledged master of the team, felt his supremacy threatened by this strange Southland dog. And strange Buck was. Other Southland dogs that Spitz had known were too soft for the trail, dying under the toil, the frost, and starvation. Buck alone endured and prospered, matching the husky in strength and cunning. And Buck was a masterful dog. He wanted leadership because it was his nature, but he wanted it also because he had been gripped by the pride of the trail and trace—that pride which holds dogs in the toil to the last gasp, and breaks their hearts if they are cut out of the harness. This was the pride that transformed dogs from sullen brutes into straining, eager creatures and spurred them on all day. This was the pride that bore up Spitz and made him thrash the dogs who blundered in the traces or hid at harness time. And it was this pride that made him fear Buck as a possible lead dog.

It now became open war between them. Buck came between Spitz and the shirks he should have punished. And he did it deliberately. One night there was a heavy snowfall, and in the morning Pike, the malingerer, did not appear. He was securely hidden in his nest under a foot of snow. François sought him in vain. Spitz was wild. He raged through the camp, smelling and digging in every likely place, snarling so frightfully that Pike shivered in his hiding place.

But when he was at last unearthed, and Spitz flew to punish him, Buck flew, with equal rage, in between. So unexpected was it, and so shrewdly managed, that Spitz was hurled backward off his feet. Pike, who had been trembling abjectly, took heart and sprang on his overthrown leader. Buck, to whom fair play was a forgotten code, likewise sprang upon Spitz. But François, chuckling yet unswerving in the administration of justice, brought his lash down on Buck with all his might, while Spitz soundly punished the offending Pike.

As Dawson grew closer, Buck continued to interfere between Spitz and the culprits; but now he did it craftily, when François was not around. Soon a general insubordination sprang up. Dave and Sol-leks were unaffected, but the rest of the team went from bad to worse. Trouble was always afoot, and at the bottom of it was Buck. François was in constant apprehension of the life-and-death struggle which he knew must take place sooner or later; and on more than one night the sounds of quarreling among the dogs turned him out of his sleeping robe, fearful that Buck and Spitz were at it.

But they pulled into crowded Dawson one dreary afternoon with the great fight still to come. Here were many men, and countless dogs, and all day and night their bells jingled as they swung up and down the main street in long teams. They hauled cabin logs and firewood, freighted up to the mines, and did all manner of work. Here and there was a Southland dog, but in the main they were the wild wolf-husky breed. Every night at regular intervals, with the aurora borealis flaming coldly overhead, or the stars leaping in the frost dance, they raised a weird and eerie chant, as old as the breed itself, in which it was Buck's delight to join.

Seven days later the team headed back again toward Dyea and Skagway. Perrault was again carrying urgent dispatches; also, the travel pride had gripped him, and he purposed to make the record trip of the year. Several things favored him. The dogs were rested and in trim. The trail was now packed hard. And the police had arranged deposits of grub in two or three places, so he was traveling light.

They made a fifty-mile run on the first day, and the second day were well on the way up the Yukon. But Buck's revolt had destroyed the solidarity of the team. It was no longer as one dog leaping in the traces. No more was Spitz a leader greatly to be feared. The rebels had grown equal to challenging his authority. And Buck was even swaggering up and down, snarling and bristling, before Spitz's very nose.

The breakdown of discipline likewise affected the dogs' relations with one another. All but Dave and Sol-leks quarreled till the camp was a howling bedlam. François swore, and stamped the snow in rage, and tore his hair. His lash was always singing, but directly his back was turned the bickering began again. He backed up Spitz with his whip, while Buck backed up the remainder of the team. François knew he was behind all the trouble, and Buck knew he knew; but Buck was too clever ever again to be caught red-handed. To work faithfully in the harness had become a delight to him; yet now it was a greater delight slyly to precipitate a fight among his mates and tangle the traces.

One night, Dub turned up a snowshoe rabbit. In a second the whole team was in full cry. A hundred yards away was a camp of the North-west Police, with fifty dogs who joined the chase down the river and up the frozen bed of a creek. The rabbit sped lightly on the surface of the snow; the dogs plowed through by main strength. Buck led the pack, whining eagerly, his splendid body flashing forward, leap by leap, in the wan, white moonlight. And leap by leap, like some pale frost wraith, the snowshoe rabbit flashed on ahead.

There is an ecstasy that marks the summit of life, beyond which life cannot rise. And this ecstasy came to Buck, sounding the old wolf cry from the deeps of his nature, as he strained after the living meat.

But Spitz, cold and calculating even in his supreme moods, left the pack and cut across a narrow neck of land where the creek made a long bend around. As Buck rounded the bend, the frost wraith still flitting before him, he saw a larger wraith leap from the overhanging bank into the rabbit's path. It was Spitz. The rabbit could not turn, and as the white teeth broke its back it shrieked as a stricken man may shriek, and the full pack at Buck's heels raised a hell's chorus of delight.

But Buck did not cry out. He did not check himself, but drove in upon Spitz, shoulder to shoulder, so hard that he missed the throat. They rolled over and over in the powdery snow. Spitz gained his feet and leaped clear, slashing Buck down the shoulder with teeth that clipped together like the steel jaws of a trap.

In a flash Buck knew it. The time had come. It was to the death. As they circled about, snarling, ears laid back, keenly watchful for the advantage, Buck seemed to remember it all—the white woods, and earth, and moonlight, and the thrill of battle. Over the whiteness

THE CALL OF THE WILD

brooded a ghostly calm. Nothing moved, not a leaf quivered, the visible breaths of the other dogs, now drawn up in a silent, expectant circle, rose slowly and lingered in the frosty air.

In vain Buck strove to sink his teeth in the neck of the big white dog. But Spitz was a practiced fighter. He had held his own with all manner of dogs. Bitter rage was his, but never blind rage. Wherever Buck's fangs struck for the flesh, they were countered by the fangs of Spitz. Time and time again Buck tried for the snow-white throat, where life bubbled near to the surface, and every time Spitz slashed and got away. Then Buck took to driving his shoulder at Spitz as a ram to overthrow him. But instead, Buck's shoulder was slashed each time as Spitz leaped lightly away.

Spitz was untouched, while Buck was streaming with blood and panting hard. The fight was growing desperate. And all the while the silent wolfish circle waited. As Buck grew winded, Spitz took to rushing, and kept him staggering for footing. Once he went over, and the whole circle of sixty dogs started up; but he recovered almost in mid-air, and the circle sank down again.

But Buck possessed a quality that made for greatness—imagination. If he fought by instinct, he could fight by head as well. He rushed, as though for the old shoulder trick, but at the last instant swept low to the snow and in. His teeth closed on Spitz's left foreleg. There was a crunch of bone, and the white dog faced him on three legs. Thrice Buck tried to knock him over, then repeated the trick and broke the right foreleg. Spitz struggled madly to keep up. He saw the gleaming eyes, the lolling tongues, and silvery breaths begin to close in upon him as he had seen similar circles close in upon beaten antagonists in the past.

Buck was inexorable. Mercy was a thing reserved for gentler climes. He maneuvered for the final rush. The circle had tightened until he could feel the breaths of the huskies on his flanks. He could see them, beyond Spitz and to either side, half crouching for the spring. A pause seemed to fall. Every animal was motionless as though turned to stone. Only Spitz quivered and staggered back and forth, snarling with horrible menace, as though to frighten off impending death. Then Buck sprang in and out; but while he was in, shoulder at last met shoulder. The dark circle became a dot on the moon-flooded snow as Spitz disappeared from view. Buck stood and looked on, the successful champion, the dominant primordial beast who had made his kill and found it good.

CHAPTER IV

"EH? WOT I SAY? I spik true w'en I say dat Buck two devils," said François next morning when he discovered Spitz missing and Buck covered with wounds.

"Dat Spitz fight lak hell," said Perrault, as he surveyed the gaping rips and cuts.

"An' dat Buck fight lak two hells," was François's answer. "An' now we make good time. No more Spitz, no more trouble."

While Perrault packed the camp outfit and loaded the sled, François proceeded to harness the dogs. Buck trotted up to the place Spitz would have occupied as leader; but François, not noticing him, brought Sol-leks to the coveted position, for in his judgment, Sol-leks was the best lead dog left. Buck sprang upon Sol-leks in a fury, driving him back and standing in his place.

"Eh? Eh?" François cried, slapping his thighs gleefully. "Look at dat Buck. Heem keel dat Spitz, heem t'ink to take de job. Go 'way, Chook!" And though Buck growled threateningly, he dragged him by the scruff of the neck to one side and replaced Sol-leks. When François turned his back, Buck again displaced Sol-leks, who showed plainly that he was afraid of Buck and not at all unwilling to go.

Francois was angry. "Now, by Gar, I feex you!" he cried, coming back with a heavy club in his hand.

Buck retreated slowly; nor did he attempt to charge in when Sol-leks was once more brought forward. But he circled just beyond the range of the club, snarling with rage; and while he circled he watched the club so as to dodge if François threw it, for he was wise in the way of clubs.

The driver went about his work, and called to Buck when he was ready to put him in his old place in front of Dave. Buck retreated two or three steps. François followed him, and he again retreated. After some time, François threw down the club, but what Buck wanted was not to escape a clubbing but to have the leadership. He had earned it, and he would not be content with less.

Perrault took a hand. Between them they ran him about for the better part of an hour. They threw clubs at him. He dodged. They cursed him, and his fathers and mothers before him, and all his seed to come after him down to the remotest generation; but he answered curse with snarl and kept just out of their reach, advertising plainly that when his desire was met, he would come in and be good.

Perrault looked at his watch and swore. They should have been on the trail an hour gone. François scratched his head, and grinned sheepishly at the courier, who shrugged his shoulders in sign that they were beaten.

Then François went up to where Sol-leks stood and called to Buck. Buck laughed, as dogs laugh, yet kept his distance. François unfastened Sol-leks's traces and put him back in his old place. The team stood harnessed to the sled and ready for the trail. There was no place for Buck save at the front. Again François called, and now Buck trotted triumphantly into position at the head of the team. His traces were fastened, and with both men running, the team dashed out onto the river trail.

The dog driver found that he had undervalued Buck. At a bound he took up the duties of leadership; and where judgment was required, and quick thinking and quick acting, he showed himself the superior even of Spitz, of whom François had never seen an equal.

But it was in giving the law and making his mates live up to it that Buck excelled. Dave and Sol-leks did not mind the change in leadership. Their business was to toil mightily in the traces; they did not care what else happened. However, the rest of the team, which had grown unruly, was surprised greatly now that Buck proceeded to lick them into shape.

Pike, who pulled at Buck's heels, and who never put an ounce more of his weight against the breastband than he was compelled to, was swiftly and repeatedly shaken for loafing; and ere the first day was done he was pulling more than ever before in his life. The first night in camp, Joe, the sour one, was punished roundly—a thing that Spitz had never succeeded in doing. Buck simply smothered him by virtue of superior weight, and cut him up till he ceased snapping and began to whine for mercy.

The general tone of the team picked up immediately. Once more the dogs leaped as one dog in the traces. At the Rink Rapids two native huskies, Teek and Koona, were added; and the celerity with which Buck broke them in took away François's breath. "Nevaire such a dog as dat Buck!" he cried. "Heem worth one t'ousand dollair, by Gar! Eh? Wot you say, Perrault?"

And Perrault nodded. He was ahead of the record already. The Thirty Mile River was coated with ice now, and they covered in one day coming back what had taken them six days going out. They made one sixty-mile dash from the foot of Lake Laberge to the Whitehorse Rapids. Then on the last night of the second week they topped White Pass and dropped down the sea slope with the lights of Skagway and of the shipping at their feet.

It was a record run. Each day for fourteen days they had averaged forty miles. Now Perrault and François were deluged with invitations to drink, while the team was the constant center of a worshipful crowd of dog busters and mushers.

Then came official orders. François and Perrault threw their arms around Buck, wept over him, and, like other men, passed out of his life for good.

A Scotch half-breed took charge of him and his mates, and in company with a dozen other dog teams he started back over the weary trail to Dawson. It was no light running now, but heavy toil each day, with a heavy load behind; for this was the mail train, carrying word from the world to the men who sought gold under the shadow of the Pole.

At Dawson they should have had a week's rest, but in two days they were off again up the Yukon, loaded with letters for the outside. The dogs were tired and in poor condition, the drivers grumbling, and to make matters worse, it snowed every day. This meant a soft trail, greater friction on the runners, and heavier pulling; yet the drivers were fair through it all, and did their best for the animals.

Each night the dogs were attended to first. They ate before the drivers ate, and no man sought his sleeping robe till he had seen to the feet of the dogs he drove. Still, their strength went down. Since the beginning of the winter they had traveled eighteen hundred miles, dragging sleds the whole weary distance; and this will tell upon the toughest. Buck kept his mates up to their work, though he too was very tired. Billee whimpered in his sleep each night. Joe was sourer than ever, and Sol-leks was unapproachable, blind side or other side.

But it was Dave who suffered most of all. Something was wrong inside, but the drivers could locate no broken bones, could not make it out. Before long, he was so weak that he was falling repeatedly in the traces, and crying out with pain. The Scotch half-breed took him out of the team, making the next dog, Sol-leks, fast to the sled. His intention was to rest Dave, letting him run free on the beaten trail behind the sled; but Dave whimpered brokenheartedly when he saw Sol-leks in the position he had served so long.

When the sled started, he would not run on the trail but floundered in the soft snow alongside Sol-leks, attacking him with his teeth, striving to leap inside his traces and get between him and the sled, and all the while whining and yelping and crying with grief and pain. The half-breed tried to drive him back on the trail with the whip; but he paid no heed, and the man had no heart to strike harder. He went on like this till exhausted. Then he fell, and lay where he fell, howling lugubriously as the long train of sleds churned by.

With the last remnant of his strength he managed to stagger along behind till the train made another stop, when he limped past the sleds to his own, where he stood again beside Sol-leks. His driver turned a moment to get a light for his pipe from the man behind. When he started the dogs again, they swung out with remarkable lack of exertion, and then stopped in surprise. The sled had not moved. Dave had bitten through both of Sol-leks's traces, and was standing directly in front of the sled in his proper place.

He pleaded with his eyes to remain there. The driver was perplexed. His comrades talked of how a dog could break its heart through being denied the work that killed it. They held it a mercy, since Dave was to die anyway, that he should die in the traces, heart-easy and content. So he was harnessed in again, and proudly he pulled, though more than once he cried out from the bite of his inward hurt. Several times he fell and was dragged in the traces, but he held out till camp that night, when his driver made a place for him by the fire. Morning found him too weak to travel. Convulsively he wormed his way toward where the team was being harnessed. But his strength left him, and he lay gasping in the snow, yearning toward his mates. They could hear him mournfully howling till they passed out of sight behind a belt of river timber.

Here the train was halted. The Scotch half-breed slowly retraced his steps to the camp they had left. The men ceased talking. A shot rang out. The man came back hurriedly. The whips snapped, the bells tinkled merrily, the sleds churned along the trail; but Buck knew, and every dog knew, what had taken place behind the belt of river trees.

⋙ CHAPTER V ⋘

THIRTY DAYS FROM THE TIME it left Dawson, the Salt Water Mail arrived at Skagway. The dogs were in a wretched state, worn out and worn down. Buck's one hundred and forty pounds had dwindled to one hundred and fifteen. Pike, the malingerer, who had so often successfully feigned a hurt leg, was now limping in earnest. Sol-leks was lame, and Dub was suffering from a wrenched shoulder blade. They were dead tired. In less than five months they had traveled twenty-five hundred miles; during the last eighteen hundred they had had but five days' rest. As they came into Skagway they could barely keep the traces taut, and on the downgrades just managed to keep out of the way of the sled.

"Mush on, poor sore feets," the driver encouraged them as they tottered down the main street. "Dis is de las'. Den we get one long res'. Eh? For sure. One bully long res'."

The drivers expected a long stopover. But so many were the men who had rushed into the Klondike, and so many were the sweethearts, wives, and kin that had not rushed in, that the congested mail was taking on Alpine proportions. There were official orders that, since dogs counted for little against dollars, the exhausted ones were to be sold and fresh ones were to take their places.

Three days passed, by which time Buck and his mates found how really weak they were. On the morning of the fourth, two men from the States bought them, harness and all, for a song. The men addressed each other as Hal and Charles. Both were manifestly out of place, and why such as they should adventure the North is part of the mystery of things that passes understanding. Charles was middle-aged, with weak and watery eyes and a mustache that twisted fiercely up, giving the lie to the limply drooping lip it concealed. Hal was a youngster of nineteen or twenty, with a big Colt's revolver and a hunting knife strapped about him on a belt that fairly bristled with cartridges. This belt was the most salient thing about him, and it advertised his sheer and unutterable callowness.

With them was a woman—Mercedes they called her—who was Charles's wife, Hal's sister.

Buck watched them apprehensively as they took down the tent and loaded the sled. There was a great deal of effort about their manner, but no method. The tent was rolled into an awkward bundle three times as large as it should have been. The tin dishes were packed away unwashed. Mercedes kept up an unbroken chattering of remonstrance and advice.

Three men from a neighboring tent looked on, grinning and winking at one another.

"You've got a right smart load as it is," said one of them; "and it's not me should tell you your business, but I wouldn't tote that tent along if I was you."

Mercedes threw up her hands in dainty dismay. "However in the world could I manage without a tent?"

"It's springtime; you won't get any more cold weather."

She shook her head, and Charles and Hal put the last odds and ends on the mountainous load.

"Think it'll ride?" one of the men asked.

"Why shouldn't it?" Charles demanded shortly.

"Oh, that's all right, that's all right. I was just a-wonderin', that is all. It seemed a mite top-heavy."

Charles turned his back and drew the lashings down as well as he could, which was not in the least well.

"An' of course the dogs can hike along all day with that contraption behind them," affirmed a second of the men.

"Certainly," said Hal, with freezing politeness, taking hold of the gee pole with one hand and swinging his whip from the other. "Mush!" he shouted. "Mush on there!"

The dogs sprang against the breastbands, strained hard for a few moments, then relaxed. They were unable to move the sled.

"The lazy brutes, I'll show them," he cried, preparing to lash out at them with the whip.

But Mercedes caught hold of the whip. "Oh, Hal, you mustn't. The poor dears! You mustn't be harsh with them, or I won't go a step."

"Precious lot you know about dogs," her brother sneered. "You've got to whip them to get anything out of them. That's their way. You ask those men."

"They're weak as water, if you want to know," said one of the men. "Plumb tuckered out. They need a rest."

"Rest be blanked," said Hal. Again his whip fell upon the dogs. They threw themselves against the breastbands, dug their feet in, and put forth all their strength. The sled held as though it were an anchor. After two efforts, they stood still, panting. The whip was still whistling savagely when one of the onlookers, who had been clenching his teeth to suppress hot speech, now spoke up: "I don't care a whoop what becomes of you, but for the dogs' sakes I just want to tell you, you can help them a mighty lot by breaking out that sled. The runners are froze fast. Throw your weight against the gee pole, right and left, and break it out."

Hal followed the advice. The overloaded sled forged ahead, Buck and his mates struggling frantically under the rain of blows. A hundred yards ahead the path turned and sloped steeply into the main street. It would have required an experienced man to keep the top-heavy sled upright, and Hal was not such a man. As they swung on the turn the sled went over, spilling half its load through the loose lashings. The dogs never stopped. The lightened sled bounded on its side behind them. Buck was raging. He broke into a run, the team following. Hal cried, "Whoa! Whoa!" But they gave no heed. He tripped and was pulled off his feet. The capsized sled ground over him, and the dogs dashed up the street, adding to the gaiety of Skagway as they scattered the remainder of the outfit along its chief thoroughfare.

Kindhearted citizens caught the dogs and gathered up the belongings. Also, they gave advice: half the load and twice the dogs, if you ever expect to reach Dawson. Unwillingly, Hal and Charles pitched tent, and overhauled the outfit. Canned goods were turned out that made men laugh, for canned goods on the Long Trail are a thing to dream about.

"Blankets for a hotel," said one of the men who laughed and helped. "Half as many is too much. Throw away that tent, and all those dishes. Good Lord, do you think you're traveling on a Pullman?"

Even cut in half there was still a formidable bulk. Charles and Hal went out in the evening and bought six Outside dogs. These, added to the six of the original team, and the huskies obtained at the Rink

Rapids on the record trip, brought the team up to fourteen. But the Outside dogs did not amount to much. Three were short-haired pointers, one was a Newfoundland, and the other two were mongrels. Buck and his comrades looked upon them with disgust, and though he speedily taught them their places and what not to do, he could not teach them what to do. They did not take kindly to trace and trail. Except for the two mongrels, they were spirit-broken by the savage environment and the ill treatment they had received. The two mongrels were without spirit at all; bones were the only things breakable about them.

With the newcomers so forlorn, and the old team so worn out, the outlook was anything but bright. The two men, however, were cheerful and proud. They were doing the thing in style, with fourteen dogs. Never had they seen a sled with as many. In the nature of Arctic travel there was a reason why fourteen dogs should not drag one sled, and that was that one sled could not carry the food for fourteen dogs. But Charles and Hal did not know this. They had worked the trip out with a pencil, so much to a dog, so many dogs, so many days. Mercedes looked over their shoulders and nodded comprehensively, it was all so very simple.

As the days went by it became apparent that these two men and the woman not only knew nothing but could not learn. They were slack in all things, without order or discipline. It took them half the night to pitch a slovenly camp, and half the morning to break that camp and get the sled loaded so sloppily that they spent the rest of the day stopping to rearrange it. Some days they were unable to get started at all.

Then Hal awoke one day to the fact that his dog food was half gone and the distance only quarter covered. So he cut down the ration and tried to increase the day's travel. His sister and brother-in-law seconded him; but they were frustrated by their own incompetence. It was a simple matter to give the dogs less food; but it was impossible to make the dogs travel faster, while their own inability to get under way earlier in the morning prevented them from traveling longer hours.

The first to go was Dub. His wrenched shoulder blade, untreated and unrested, went from bad to worse, till finally Hal shot him with the big Colt's revolver.

The next were the six newcomers. It is a saying of the country that an untrained Outside dog starves to death on the ration of the husky, so they could do no less than die on half that ration.

By this time, shorn of its glamour, Arctic travel had become to the three Southlanders a reality too harsh to bear. The wonderful patience of the trail which comes to men who toil hard and suffer sore, and remain sweet of speech and kindly, did not come to them. They had no inkling of such a patience. They were stiff and in pain; their muscles ached, their bones ached, their very hearts ached; they became sharp of speech, and hard words were first on their lips in the morning and last at night.

Charles and Hal each cherished and often voiced the belief that he did more than his share of the work. Sometimes Mercedes sided with her husband, sometimes with her brother. The result was an unending family quarrel. And Mercedes nursed her own special grievance. She was pretty and soft, and had been chivalrously treated all her days. It was her custom to be helpless; and because she was sore and tired, she persisted in riding on the sled—a lusty last straw to the weak and starving animals. She would ride till they fell in the traces and the sled stood still. Charles and Hal would beg her to get off and walk, while she wept and importuned Heaven with their brutality.

On one occasion they took her off the sled by main strength. They never did it again. She let her legs go limp like a spoiled child, and sat down on the trail. They went on their way, but she did not move. After they had traveled three miles they unloaded the sled, came back for her, and lifted her on again.

Through it all Buck staggered along at the head of the team as in a nightmare. He pulled when he could; when he could no longer pull, he fell down and remained down till blows from whip or club drove him to his feet again. All the stiffness and gloss had gone out of his beautiful furry coat. The hair hung down, limp and draggled, or matted with dried blood where Hal's club had bruised him. His muscles had wasted away to knotty strings; each rib and every bone in his frame were outlined through the loose hide that was wrinkled in folds of emptiness. It was heartbreaking, only Buck's heart was unbreakable.

Six remaining mates, like him, were bags of bones in which sparks of life fluttered faintly. When a halt was made, they dropped in the traces, and the spark dimmed and seemed to go out. When the club fell upon them, the spark fluttered feebly up, and they tottered on.

There came a day when Billee, the good-natured, fell and could not rise. The next day Koona went, and but five remained: Joe, too far gone to be malignant; limping Pike, no longer conscious enough to malinger; Sol-leks, the one-eyed, still faithful to the toil of trace and trail; Teek, who had not traveled so far that winter and who was now beaten more than the others because he was fresher; and Buck, still at the head of the team, but no longer enforcing discipline, blind with weakness and keeping the trail by the dim feel of his feet.

It was beautiful spring weather, but neither dogs nor humans were aware of it. It was dawn by three in the morning, and twilight lingered till nine at night. The whole long day was a blaze of sunshine. A great spring murmur arose from all the land, fraught with the joy of living. The sap was rising in the pines. The willows and aspens were bursting out in young buds. Crickets sang in the nights, and in the days partridges and woodpeckers boomed in the forest. Squirrels were chattering while the wildfowl, driving up from the South, honked overhead.

From every slope came the trickle of running water, the music of unseen fountains. All things were thawing, bending, snapping. The Yukon was straining to break loose the ice that bound it down. The current ate away from beneath; the sun ate from above. Air holes formed, fissures sprang and spread apart, while thin sections of ice fell through bodily into the river. And amid all this bursting, rending, throbbing of awakening life, like wayfarers to death, staggered the two men, the woman, and their team.

With the dogs falling, Mercedes weeping and riding, Hal swearing, and Charles's eyes wistfully watering, they came to John Thornton's camp at the mouth of White River. When they halted, the dogs dropped down as though they had all been struck dead. Mercedes dried her eyes and looked at John Thornton. Charles sat down slowly and painfully on a log to rest. Hal did the talking. John Thornton was whittling the last touches on an axe handle he had made from a stick of birch. He whittled and listened, and, when it was asked, gave terse advice. He knew the breed, and he gave his advice in the certainty that it would not be followed.

"They told us up above that the bottom was dropping out of the trail and that the best thing for us to do was to lay over," Hal said, in response to Thornton's warning to take no more chances on the rotten ice. "They told us we couldn't make White River, and here we are." This last with a sneering ring of triumph in it.

"And they told you true," John Thornton answered. "The bottom's likely to drop out at any moment. Only fools, with the blind luck of fools, could have made it. I tell you straight, I wouldn't risk my carcass on that ice for all the gold in Alaska."

"That's because you're not a fool, I suppose," said Hal. "All the same, we'll go on to Dawson." He uncoiled his whip. "Get up there, Buck! Hi! Get up there! Mush on!"

Thornton went on whittling. It was idle, he knew, to get between a fool and his folly; two or three fools more or less would not alter the scheme of things.

But the dogs did not get up at the command, so the whip flashed out on its merciless errands. John Thornton compressed his lips. Sol-leks was the first to crawl to his feet. Teek followed. Joe came next, yelping with pain. Pike made two painful attempts, and on the third managed to rise. Buck made no effort. He lay where he had fallen. The lash bit into him again and again, but he neither whined nor struggled. Several times Thornton started, as though to speak, but changed his mind. A moisture came into his eyes, and, as the whipping continued, he arose and walked irresolutely up and down.

This was the first time Buck had failed, in itself a sufficient reason to drive Hal into a rage. He exchanged the whip for the club, but Buck refused to move under the rain of heavier blows. Like his mates, he was barely able to get up, but, unlike them, he had made up his mind not to. What with the thin and rotten ice he had felt under his feet all day, it seemed that he sensed disaster out there on the ice where his master was trying to drive him. As the blows continued to fall, the spark of life within flickered and nearly went out. Very faintly he could hear the impact of the club upon his body. But it was no longer his body, it seemed so far away.

And then, suddenly, with a cry like an animal, John Thornton sprang upon the man who wielded the club and hurled him backward. Mercedes screamed. Charles looked on through his watery eyes, but did not get up.

John Thornton stood over Buck, for the moment too convulsed with rage to speak.

"If you strike this dog again, I'll kill you," he said at last in a choking voice.

"It's my dog," Hal replied, wiping the blood from his mouth. "Get out of my way, or I'll fix you. I'm going to Dawson."

Thornton, axe in hand, stood between him and Buck, and evinced no intention of moving. Hal drew his long hunting knife. Mercedes screamed hysterically. Thornton rapped Hal's knuckles with the axe handle, knocking the knife to the ground. Then he stooped and picked it up, and with two strokes cut Buck's traces.

Hal had no fight left in him. Besides, Buck was too nearly dead to be of further use. A few minutes later they pulled out from the bank and down the river. Buck heard them go and raised his head to see. Pike was leading, Sol-leks at the wheel, and between were Joe and Teek. They were limping and staggering. Mercedes was riding the loaded sled. Hal guided at the gee pole, and Charles pushed and stumbled in the rear.

As Buck looked after them, Thornton knelt beside him and with rough, kindly hands searched for broken bones. By the time his search had disclosed nothing more than many bruises and a state of terrible starvation, the sled was a quarter of a mile away. Dog and man watched it crawling along over the ice. Suddenly, they saw its back end drop down, as into a rut, and the gee pole, with Hal clinging to it, jerk into the air. They heard Mercedes scream, saw Charles turn to run back, and then a whole section of ice give way and dogs and humans disappear. A yawning hole was all that was to be seen. The bottom had dropped out of the trail.

John Thornton and Buck looked at each other.

"You poor devil," said John Thornton, and Buck licked his hand.

CHAPTER VI

WHEN JOHN THORNTON froze his feet the previous December, his partners had made him comfortable and left him to get well, going on themselves up the river to get out a raft of logs for the sawmill at Dawson. He still had a slight limp when he rescued Buck, but with the warm weather even this left him. And here, lying by the river through the long spring days, watching the running water, listening lazily to the songs of birds and the hum of nature, Buck slowly won back his strength.

It must be confessed that Buck waxed lazy as his wounds healed, his muscles swelled out, and the flesh came back to cover his bones. For that matter, they were all loafing—Buck, John Thornton, and Skeet and Nig—waiting for the raft to come to carry them down to Dawson. Skeet was a little Irish setter who made friends with Buck when he was almost dying. Regularly each morning she washed and cleansed his wounds, till he came to look for her ministrations as much as he did for Thornton's. Nig, equally friendly, though less demonstrative, was a huge black dog, half bloodhound and half deerhound, with eyes that laughed and a boundless good nature.

Neither dog showed jealousy of Buck. They seemed to share the kindliness and largeness of John Thornton. As Buck grew stronger they enticed him into all sorts of ridiculous games, in which Thornton joined, and in this fashion Buck romped through convalescence into a new existence.

Love, genuine passionate love, was his for the first time. Friendship he had experienced at Judge Miller's down in the sun-kissed Santa Clara Valley. But love that was feverish and burning, that was adoration, that was madness, it had taken John Thornton to arouse.

This man had saved his life, which was something; but, further, he was the ideal master. He saw to the welfare of his dogs as if they were his own children; and to sit down for a long talk with them (gas, he called it) was as much his delight as theirs. He had a way of taking Buck's head between his hands, and resting his own head upon Buck's, of shaking him back and forth, the while calling him ill names that to Buck were love names. Buck knew no greater joy than that rough embrace and the sound of murmured oaths. When, released, he sprang to his feet, his mouth laughing, his eyes eloquent, his throat vibrant with unuttered sound, John Thornton would reverently exclaim, "God! You can all but speak!"

Buck had a trick of love expression that was akin to hurt. He would seize Thornton's hand in his mouth and close so fiercely that the flesh bore the impress of his teeth for some time afterward. And as Buck understood the oaths to be love words, so the man understood this feigned bite for a caress.

For a long time after his rescue, Buck did not like Thornton to get out of his sight. From the moment he left the tent to when he entered it again, Buck would follow at his heels. He would lie by the hour at Thornton's feet, looking up into his face, studying each fleeting expression. Or, as chance might have it, he would lie to the side or rear, watching the outlines of the man and the occasional movements of his body. And often, such was the communion in which they lived, the strength of Buck's gaze would draw John Thornton's head around, and he would return the gaze, without speech, his heart shining out of his eyes as Buck's heart shone out.

But in spite of Buck's great love, the primitive strain which the

Northland had aroused in him remained alive and active. Faithfulness and devotion were his, yet he was a thing of the wild, come in from the wild to sit by John Thornton's fire. Because of his love, he could not steal from this man; but from any other man, in any other camp, he did not hesitate an instant, with a cunning which enabled him to escape detection.

He fought as fiercely as ever. Skeet and Nig were too good-natured to quarrel—besides, they belonged to John Thornton; but a strange dog, no matter what the breed or valor, swiftly acknowledged Buck's supremacy or found himself struggling for life. For Buck was merciless. He had learned well the law of club and fang. He must master or be mastered. In the primordial life, mercy was misunderstood for fear; and such misunderstandings made for death. Master or be mastered; kill or be killed, eat or be eaten, was the law; which, down out of the depths of Time, he obeyed.

He was older than the days he had seen and the breaths he had drawn. He sat by John Thornton's fire, a broad-breasted dog, white-fanged and long-furred; but behind him were the shades of all manner of dogs, half wolves and wild wolves, urgent and prompting, tasting the savor of the meat he ate, scenting the wind with him, dreaming with him and beyond him and becoming themselves the stuff of his dreams.

So peremptorily did these shades beckon him, that each day mankind and the claims of mankind slipped farther from him. Deep in the forest a call was sounding, and as often as he heard this call, he felt compelled to turn his back upon the fire and the beaten earth around it, and to plunge into the forest, and on and on, he knew not where or why. But as often as he gained the soft unbroken earth and the green shade, the love for John Thornton drew him back to the fire again.

Thornton alone held him. The rest of mankind was as nothing. When Thornton's partners, Hans and Pete, arrived on the long-expected raft, Buck refused to notice them till he learned they were close to Thornton; after that he tolerated them in a passive sort of way, accepting favors as though he favored them by accepting. They were of the same large type as Thornton, living close to the earth, thinking simply and seeing clearly; and before they swung the raft into the big eddy by the sawmill at Dawson, they understood Buck and his ways.

Thornton alone could put a pack upon Buck's back in the summer traveling, and nothing was too great for Buck to do when Thornton commanded.

"I'm not hankering to be the man that lays hands on John while Buck's around," Pete said one day.

"Py Jingo!" was Hans's contribution. "Not mineself either."

It was at Circle City, before the year was out, that Pete's apprehensions were realized. "Black" Burton, a man evil-tempered and malicious, had been picking a quarrel with a tenderfoot at the bar, when Thornton stepped good-naturedly between. Buck was lying, head on paws, watching his master's every action. Burton struck out, without warning, straight from the shoulder. Thornton was sent spinning, and stopped himself from falling only by clutching the rail of the bar.

With a roar, Buck rose in the air for Burton's throat. The man saved his life by throwing out his arm, but was hurled backward to the floor with Buck on top of him. Buck loosed his teeth from the arm and drove in again for the throat, this time tearing it open. Then the crowd was upon Buck, and he was driven off; but while a surgeon checked the bleeding, he prowled up and down, growling furiously, attempting to rush in, and being forced back by an array of hostile clubs. A "miners' meeting," called on the spot, decided that the dog had had sufficient provocation, and Buck was discharged. But his reputation was made, and from that day his name spread through every camp in Alaska.

In the fall of the year, he saved John Thornton's life, but in quite another fashion. The three partners were lining a long and narrow poling-boat down a bad stretch of rapids on the Forty Mile Creek. Hans and Pete moved along the bank, snubbing with a thin Manila rope from tree to tree, while Thornton poled in the boat and shouted directions to the shore.

Buck, on the bank, worried and anxious, kept abreast, his eyes never off his master.

At a particularly bad spot a ledge of barely submerged rocks jutted out from the bank into the river, and Hans let out the rope. Thornton poled the boat out into the stream, and Hans ran down the bank with the end of the rope in his hand to snub the boat when it had cleared the ledge. This it did, and it was flying downstream in a current as swift as a millrace when Hans checked with the rope; but he checked too suddenly. The boat flirted over, and Thornton, flung sheer out of it, was carried downstream toward the worst of the rapids, a stretch of wild water in which no swimmer could live.

Buck had sprung in on the instant; and at the end of three hundred yards, amid a mad swirl of water, he overhauled Thornton. When he felt him grasp his tail, Buck swam for the bank with all his splendid strength. But the progress shoreward was slow, the progress downstream amazingly rapid. From below came the fatal roaring where the wild current went wilder and was rent in shreds and spray by rocks thrust up like the teeth of an enormous comb. The suck of the water at the top of the last steep pitch was frightful, and Thornton knew that the shore was impossible. He scraped furiously over a rock, bruised across a second, and struck a third with crushing force. He clutched its slippery top with both hands, releasing Buck, and above the churning water shouted: "Go, Buck! Go!"

Buck, struggling desperately, could not hold his own, and swept on downstream. When he heard Thornton's command repeated, he partly reared out of the water, throwing his head high, then turned obediently toward the bank. He was dragged ashore by Pete and Hans at the very point where swimming ceased to be possible and destruction began.

They knew no man could cling to a slippery rock in the face of that current for more than a few minutes, and they ran up the bank to a point far above where Thornton was hanging on. Attaching the snub line carefully to Buck's neck and shoulders, they launched him into the stream. There, the faint sound of Thornton's voice came to him, and he knew that his master was in his extremity. He struck out boldly, straight into the stream. Hans paid out the rope, permitting no slack, while Pete kept it clear of coils. Buck held on till he was on a line straight above Thornton; then he turned, and with the speed of an express train headed down upon him.

Thornton saw him coming, and, as Buck struck him like a battering ram, with the whole force of the current behind him, he reached up and closed with both arms around the shaggy neck. Hans snubbed the rope around the tree, and Buck and Thornton were jerked under the water. Strangling, suffocating, sometimes one uppermost and sometimes the other, dragging over the jagged bottom, smashing against rocks and snags, they veered in to the bank.

Thornton came to, belly downward, being violently propelled back and forth across a drift log by Hans and Pete. His first glance on recovering was for Buck, over whose limp body Nig was setting up a howl, while Skeet was licking the wet face and closed eyes. Slowly Buck was brought around, and Thornton, himself bruised and battered, went carefully over him and found three broken ribs.

"That settles it," Thornton announced. "We camp right here." And camp they did, till Buck's ribs knitted and he was able to travel.

That winter, at Dawson, Buck performed another exploit, not so heroic, perhaps, but one that put his name many notches higher on the totem pole of Alaskan fame. It began in the Eldorado Saloon, where men waxed boastful of their favorite dogs. Buck, because of his record, was the target, and Thornton was driven to defend him. Finally one man stated that his dog could start a sled with five hundred pounds and walk off with it; a second bragged six hundred for his dog; and a third, seven hundred.

"Pooh! Pooh!" said Thornton. "Buck can start a thousand pounds."

"And break it out! And walk off with it for a hundred yards?" demanded Matthewson, a Bonanza king, he of the seven-hundred vaunt.

"And break it out, and walk off with it for a hundred yards," Thornton said coolly.

"Well," Matthewson said slowly, "I've got a thousand dollars that says he can't. And there it is." He slammed a sack of gold dust the size of a bologna sausage down upon the bar.

Nobody spoke. Thornton could feel a flush of warm blood creeping up his face. His tongue had tricked him. He did not know whether Buck could start a thousand pounds. Half a ton! The enormousness of it appalled him. Further, he had no thousand dollars; nor had Hans or Pete.

"I've got a sled standing outside now, with twenty fifty-pound sacks of flour on it," Matthewson went on with brutal directness, "so don't let that hinder you."

Thornton did not reply. He glanced from face to face in the absent way of a man who has lost the power of thought. The face of Jim O'Brien, a king of the Mastodon gold strike and old-time comrade, caught his eyes. It roused him to do what he would never have dreamed of doing.

"Can you lend me a thousand?" he asked in a whisper.

"Sure," answered O'Brien, thumping down a bulging sack beside Matthewson's. "Though it's little faith I'm having, John, that the beast can do the trick."

The Eldorado emptied its occupants into the street to see the test. Several hundred men, furred and mittened, banked around Matthewson's sled. Loaded with a thousand pounds of flour, it had been standing for a couple of hours, and in the intense cold (it was sixty below zero) the runners had frozen fast to the hard-packed snow. Men offered odds of two to one that Buck could not budge it.

A quibble arose concerning the phrase "break out." O'Brien contended it was Thornton's privilege to knock the runners loose, leaving Buck to "break it out" from a dead standstill. Matthewson insisted that the phrase included breaking the runners from the frozen grip of the snow. A majority of the men decided in his favor, and the odds against Buck went up to three to one.

There were no takers. Not a man believed he could do it. As Thornton looked at the sled, with its regular team of ten dogs curled up in the snow before it, the test appeared impossible. Matthewson waxed jubilant.

"Three to one!" he proclaimed. "I'll lay you another thousand at that figure, Thornton. What d'ye say?"

Thornton's doubt was strong in his face, but his fighting spirit was aroused. He called Hans and Pete. The three partners could rake together only two hundred dollars, their total capital; yet they laid it unhesitatingly against Matthewson's six hundred.

The sled team was unhitched, and Buck, with his own harness, was put into the sled. He had caught the excitement, and felt that he must do a great thing for John Thornton. Murmurs of admiration at his splendid appearance went up. He was in perfect condition, without an ounce of superfluous flesh, and the one hundred and fifty pounds that he now weighed were so many pounds of grit and virility. His furry coat shone with the sheen of silk. Men felt his muscles and proclaimed them hard as iron, and the odds went down to two to one.

"Gad, sir! Gad, sir!" stuttered a king of the Skookum Benches. "I offer you eight hundred for him, sir, before the test, sir; eight hundred just as he stands."

Thornton shook his head and stepped to Buck's side.

"You must stand off from him," Matthewson protested. "Free play and plenty of room."

The crowd fell silent. Thornton knelt down and took Buck's head in his two hands and rested cheek to cheek. "As you love me, Buck. As you love me," he whispered. Buck had caught the excitement, and he whined with suppressed eagerness.

The crowd was watching curiously. The affair was growing mysterious. It seemed like conjuring. As Thornton got to his feet, Buck seized his mittened hand between his jaws, pressing in with his teeth and releasing slowly, half reluctantly. It was his answer. Thornton stepped well back.

"Now, Buck," he said.

Buck tightened the traces, then slacked them for several inches.

"Gee!" Thornton's voice rang out, sharp in the tense silence.

Buck swung to the right, ending the movement in a plunge that took up the slack and with a sudden jerk arrested his one hundred and fifty pounds. The load quivered, and from under the runners arose a crisp crackling.

"Haw!" Thornton commanded.

Buck duplicated the maneuver, this time to the left. The crackling turned into a snapping, the sled pivoting and the runners slipping and grating several inches to the side. The sled was broken out. Men were unconsciously holding their breaths.

"Now, MUSH!"

Thornton's command cracked out like a pistol shot. Buck threw himself forward, tightening the traces with a jarring lunge. His whole body gathered compactly together in the tremendous effort, muscles writhing and knotting like live things under the silky fur. His great chest was low to the ground, his head forward and down, his feet were flying like mad, the claws scarring the hard-packed snow in parallel grooves. The sled swayed and trembled, half started forward. One of his feet slipped, and one man groaned aloud. Then the sled lurched ahead in what appeared a rapid succession of jerks, though it never really came to a dead stop again . . . half an inch . . . an inch . . . two inches. . . . The jerks perceptibly diminished; as the sled gained momentum, he caught them up, till it was moving steadily along.

Men gasped and began to breathe again. Thornton ran behind, encouraging Buck with short, cheery words. The distance had been measured off, and as he neared the pile of firewood which marked the end of the hundred yards, a cheer began to grow and grow, which burst into a roar as he passed the mark and halted at command. Every man was tearing himself loose, even Matthewson. Hats and mittens were flying in the air. Men were shaking hands, it did not matter with whom, and bubbling over in a general incoherent babel.

But Thornton fell on his knees beside Buck. Head was against head, and he was shaking him back and forth. Those who hurried up heard him cursing Buck, and he cursed him long and fervently, and softly and lovingly.

"Gad sir! Gad, sir!" spluttered the Skookum Bench king. "I'll give you a thousand for him, sir, a thousand, sir—twelve hundred, sir."

Thornton rose to his feet. His eyes were wet. The tears were streaming frankly down his cheeks. "Sir," he said to the Skookum Bench king, "no, sir. You can go to hell, sir. It's the best I can do for you, sir."

Buck seized Thornton's hand in his teeth. Thornton shook him back and forth. As though animated by a common impulse, the onlookers drew back to a respectful distance; nor were they again indiscreet enough to interrupt.

CHAPTER VII

WHEN BUCK EARNED sixteen hundred dollars in five minutes for John Thornton, he made it possible for his master to pay off certain debts and to journey with his partners into the East after a fabled lost mine. Many men had sought it; and more than a few had never returned from the quest. Dying men, clinching their testimony with nuggets that were unlike any known grade of gold in the Northland, had sworn the mine existed, its site marked by an ancient and ramshackle cabin.

But no man still alive had looted this treasure house, and the dead were dead; wherefore John Thornton and Pete and Hans, with Buck and half a dozen other dogs, faced into the East to achieve where men and dogs as good as themselves had failed.

John Thornton asked little of man or nature. With a handful of salt and a rifle he could plunge into the wilderness and fare wherever he pleased. Being in no haste, Indian fashion, he hunted his dinner in the course of the day's travel; and if he failed to find it, like the Indian he kept on traveling, secure in the knowledge that sooner or later he would come to it. So, on this great journey into the East, straight meat was the bill of fare, ammunition and tools principally made up the load on the sled, and the time card was drawn upon the limitless future.

To Buck it was boundless delight, this hunting, fishing, and indefinite wandering through strange places. For weeks at a time they would hold on steadily, day after day; and for weeks upon end they would camp, the dogs loafing and the men burning holes through frozen muck and gravel and washing countless pans of dirt by the heat of the fire. Sometimes they went hungry, sometimes they feasted riotously, all according to the abundance of game, and the fortune of hunting.

The months came and went, and back and forth they twisted through the uncharted vastness, where no men were and yet where men had been if the Lost Cabin were true. Under the midnight sun, in the shadows of glaciers, they picked strawberries and flowers as ripe and fair as any the Southland could boast. In the fall of the year they penetrated a weird lake country, sad and silent, where wildfowl had been, but where then there was no life nor sign of life—only the blowing of chill winds, the forming of ice in sheltered places, and the melancholy rippling of waves on lonely beaches.

And through another winter they wandered on. Once they came upon an ancient path blazed through the forest, and the Lost Cabin seemed very near. But the path began nowhere and ended nowhere. Another time they chanced upon the time-graven wreckage of a hunting lodge, and amid the shreds of rotted blankets John Thornton found a long-barreled flintlock. He knew it for a Hudson's Bay Company gun of the young days in the Northwest, when such a gun was worth its height in beaver skins packed flat. And that was all—no hint as to the man who in an early day had reared the lodge and left the gun among the blankets.

Spring came on once more, and at the end of all their wandering they found, not the Lost Cabin, but a shallow placer in a broad valley where the gold showed like yellow butter across the bottom of the washing pan. They sought no farther. Each day they worked earned them thousands of dollars in clean dust and nuggets, and they worked every day. The gold was sacked in moose-hide bags, fifty pounds to the bag, and piled like so much firewood outside their spruce-bough lodge. Like giants they toiled, days flashing on the heels of days like dreams as they heaped the treasure up.

There was nothing for the dogs to do, save now and again to haul in the meat that Thronton killed, and Buck spent long hours musing by the fire.

But the call was still sounding for him in the depths of the forest. It awoke in him wild yearnings and stirrings for he knew not what. Irresistible impulses seized him. He would be lying in camp, dozing lazily, when suddenly his head would lift and his ears cock, intent and listening, and he would spring to his feet and dash away for hours, through the forest aisles and across the open spaces. He loved to run down dry water-courses, and to spy upon the birdlife in the woods. For a day at a time he would lie in the underbrush where he could watch the partridges drumming and strutting up and down. But especially he loved to run in the dim twilight of the late summer midnights, listening to the subdued and sleepy murmurs of the forest, reading signs and sounds as man may read a book, and seeking for the mysterious something that called—called, waking or sleeping, at all times, for him to come.

One night he sprang from sleep with a start, eager-eyed, nostrils quivering and scenting, his mane bristling in recurrent waves. From the forest came the call (or one note of it, for the call was many-noted), distinct and definite as never before—a long-drawn howl, like, yet unlike, any noise made by husky dog. And he knew it as a sound heard before. He sprang through the sleeping camp and in swift silence dashed through the woods. As he drew closer to the cry he went more slowly, with caution in every movement, till he came to an open place among the trees, and looking out saw, erect on haunches, with nose pointed to the sky, a long and lean and gray timber wolf.

He had made no noise, yet it sensed his presence and ceased its howling. Buck stalked into the open, half crouching, body gathered compactly together, tail straight and stiff, feet falling with unwonted care. Every movement commingled threat and friendliness. It was the menacing truce that marks the meeting of wild beasts that prey. But the wolf fled at sight of him. He followed, with wild leapings, in a frenzy to overtake. He ran him into a blind channel, in the bed of the creek, where a timber jam barred the way. The wolf whirled, pivoting on his hind legs like any cornered husky dog, snarling and bristling, clipping his teeth together in a rapid succession of snaps.

Buck did not attack, but circled him about and hedged him in with friendly advances. The wolf was suspicious and afraid; for Buck made three of him in weight, while his head barely reached Buck's shoulder. Watching his chance, he darted away, and the chase was resumed. Time and again he was cornered, and the thing repeated, but in the end Buck's pertinacity was rewarded. The wolf sniffed noses with him, and soon they played about in the nervous, half-coy way with which fierce beasts belie their fierceness. After some time of this the wolf started off at an easy lope in a manner that plainly showed he was going somewhere. He made it clear to Buck that he was to come, and they ran side by side through the somber twilight, straight up the creek bed, into the gorge from which it issued, and across the bleak divide.

On the opposite slope of the watershed they came down into a level country where were great stretches of forest and many streams, and through these stretches they ran hour after hour, as the sun rose and the day grew warm. Buck was wildly glad. He knew he was at last answering the call, running by the side of his wood brother toward the place from where the call surely came.

They stopped by a running stream to drink, and, stopping, Buck remembered John Thornton. He sat down. The wolf started on, then returned to him, sniffing noses and making actions as though to encourage him. But Buck turned about and started slowly on the back track. For the better part of an hour the wild brother ran by his side, whining softly. Then he sat down, pointed his nose upward, and howled. It was a mournful howl, and as Buck held steadily on his way he heard it grow faint and fainter until it was lost in the distance.

John Thornton was eating dinner when Buck dashed into camp and sprang upon him in a frenzy of affection, overturning him, scrambling upon him, licking his face, biting his hand—"playing the general tomfool," as John Thornton characterized it, the while he shook Buck back and forth and cursed him lovingly.

For two days and nights Buck never left camp, never let Thornton out of his sight. But after two days his restlessness came back. Again he took to wandering in the woods, but the wild brother came no more; and though he listened through long vigils, the mournful howl was never raised.

He began to sleep out at night, and once he crossed the divide and wandered for a week, killing his meat as he went and traveling with the long, easy lope that seems never to tire. He fished for salmon in a broad stream that emptied somewhere into the sea, and by this stream he killed a large black bear. It was a hard fight, and aroused all his latent ferocity. Two days later, he returned and found a dozen wolverines quarreling over his kill. He scattered them like chaff; and those that fled left two behind who would quarrel no more.

The blood longing became stronger than ever before. He was a killer, a thing that preyed, living on the things that lived by virtue of his own strength and prowess, surviving triumphantly in a hostile world where only the strong survived. He became possessed of a great pride which advertised itself in the play of every muscle, spoke plainly as speech in the way he carried himself. But for the stray brown on his muzzle and above his eyes, and for the splash of white hair that ran down his chest, he might well have been mistaken for a gigantic wolf, with the size of his St. Bernard father and the shape of his shepherd mother.

A carnivorous animal, as formidable as any that roamed the wild, he was at the high tide of his life, overspilling with vigor and virility. When Thornton passed a caressing hand along his back, a snapping and crackling followed the hand, each hair discharging its pent magnetism at the contact. His muscles were surcharged with vitality, and snapped into play like steel springs. Life streamed through him in splendid flood, glad and rampant, until it seemed that it would burst him asunder in sheer ecstasy.

"Never was there such a dog," said John Thornton one day, as the partners watched Buck marching out of camp.

"When he was made, the mold was broke," said Pete.

"Py Jingo! I t'ink so mineself," Hans affirmed.

They saw him marching out of camp, but they did not see the instant and terrible transformation which took place within the secrecy of the forest. He no longer marched. He became a thing of the wild, stealing catfooted among the shadows. He could take a ptarmigan from its nest, kill a rabbit as it slept, and snap in midair the little chipmunks fleeing a second too late for the trees. Fish, in open pools, were not too quick for him; nor were beaver, mending their dams, too wary. He killed to eat, not from wantonness; but he preferred to eat what he killed himself. So a lurking humor ran through his deeds, and it was his delight to steal upon the squirrels, and, when he all but had them, to let them go, chattering in mortal fear to the treetops.

As fall came on, the moose moved slowly down to meet the winter in the lower and less rigorous valleys. Buck had already dragged down a stray part-grown calf; but he wished for larger quarry. He came, one day, upon a band of twenty moose, and chief among them was a great, savage bull, standing over six feet high, and as formidable an antagonist as ever Buck could desire. At the sight of Buck, he roared with fury; his great palmated antlers, branching to fourteen points and embracing seven feet within the tips, swung to and fro, and his small eyes burned, vicious and bitter.

From the bull's side, just forward of the flank, protruded a feathered arrow end, which accounted for his savageness. Guided by instinct, Buck proceeded to cut the bull out from the herd. It was no slight task. He would bark and dance about in front of him, just out of reach of the great antlers and of the terrible splay hoofs which could have stamped his life out with a single blow. The bull was driven into paroxysms of rage. He charged Buck, who retreated craftily, luring him on. But when he was thus separated from his fellows, two or three of the younger bulls would charge back upon Buck and enable the wounded chief to rejoin the herd.

There is a patience, dogged and tireless, that belongs to wildlife when it hunts its living food; and it belonged to Buck as he clung to the flank of the herd, enveloping it in a whirlwind of menace, cutting out his victim as fast as it rejoined its mates, wearing out the patience of creatures preyed upon, which is less than that of creatures preying. As the day wore along, the young bulls retraced their steps more and more reluctantly to aid their beset leader. The downcoming winter was harrying the herd on to the lower levels, and unless they left their threatened member behind, it seemed they could never shake off this tireless creature that held them back. In the end they were content to pay the toll.

As twilight fell the old bull stood with lowered head, watching his mates as they shambled off at a rapid pace through the fading light. He could not follow, for before his nose leaped the merciless fanged terror that would not let him go. Three hundredweight more than half a ton he weighed; he had lived a long, strong life, full of fight and struggle, and at the end he faced death at the teeth of a creature whose head did not reach beyond his great knuckled knees.

From then on, night and day, Buck never left his prey, never gave it a moment's rest, never permitted it to browse the leaves of trees or the shoots of young birch and willow. Nor to slake its burning thirst in the trickling streams they crossed. Often, in desperation, the bull burst into long stretches of flight. Buck did not attempt to stay him, but loped easily at his heels, satisfied with the way the game was played, lying down when the moose stood still, attacking him fiercely when he strove to eat or drink.

The great head drooped more and more under its trees of horns, and the shambling trot grew weaker and weaker. At last, at the end of the fourth day, Buck pulled the great moose down. For a day and a night he remained by the kill, eating and sleeping, turn and turn about. Then, rested, refreshed and strong, he turned his face toward camp and John Thornton, heading straight home through strange country with a certitude of direction that put man and his magnetic needle to shame.

47

As he loped on he became conscious of a new and mysterious stir in the land. There was life abroad in it different from the life which had been there. The birds talked of it, the squirrels chattered about it, the very breeze whispered of it. Several times he stopped and drew in the fresh morning air in great sniffs, reading a message which sped him on, oppressed with a sense of calamity.

Three miles from camp he came upon a fresh trail that sent his neck hair bristling. He hurried on, swiftly and stealthily, every nerve straining and tense. Suddenly his nose was jerked to the side as though a positive force had gripped it. He followed the scent into a thicket and found Nig. He was lying on his side, dead where he had dragged himself, an arrow protruding, head and feathers, from either side of his body.

A hundred yards farther on, one of the sled dogs was thrashing about in a death struggle, but Buck passed him without stopping. From the camp came the sound of many voices, rising and falling in a singsong chant. Bellying forward to the edge of the clearing, he found Hans, lying on his face, feathered with arrows like a porcupine. And then he saw what made his hair leap straight up on his neck and shoulders. A gust of rage swept over him. He growled aloud with a terrible ferocity. For the last time in his life he allowed passion to usurp cunning and reason, and it was because of his great love for John Thornton that he lost his head.

The Yeehats were dancing about the wreckage of the spruce-bough lodge when they heard a fearful roaring and saw rushing upon them an animal the like of which they had never seen before. Buck, a hurricane of fury, hurled himself on them in a frenzy to destroy. He sprang at the foremost man (it was the chief of the Yeehats), ripping the throat wide open till the jugular spouted a fountain of blood. With the next bound he tore wide the throat of a second man. There was no withstanding him. So inconceivably rapid were his movements, and so closely were the Indians tangled together, that they shot one another with arrows aimed at Buck. One young hunter, hurling a spear at him in midair, drove it through the chest of another.

Then a panic seized the Yeehats, and they fled in terror to the woods, proclaiming as they fled the advent of the Evil Spirit.

And truly Buck was the Fiend Incarnate, raging at their heels and dragging them down like deer as they raced through the trees. It was a fateful day for the Yeehats. They scattered far and wide over the country, and it was not till a week later that the last of the survivors gathered together and counted their losses.

As for Buck, wearying of the pursuit, he returned to the desolated camp. He found Pete where he had been killed in his blankets in the first moment of surprise. Thornton's desperate struggle was fresh-written on the earth, and Buck scented every detail of it down to the edge of a deep pool. By the edge, head and forefeet in the water, lay Skeet, faithful to the last. The pool itself, muddy from the miners' sluice boxes, effectually hid what it contained, and it contained John Thornton; for Buck followed his trace into the water, from which no trace led away.

All day Buck brooded by the pool or roamed restlessly about the camp. At times, when he paused to contemplate the Yeehat carcasses, he forgot the pain in a pride greater than any he had yet experienced. He had killed man, the noblest game of all, and he had killed in the face of the law of club and fang. He sniffed the bodies curiously. They had died so easily. It was harder to kill a husky dog than them.

Night came on, and a full moon bathed the land in ghostly light. Mourning by the pool, Buck became aware of a faint, sharp yelp, followed by a chorus of similar sharp yelps. They grew closer and louder. He walked to the center of the open space and listened. It was the call, the many-noted call, more luring and compelling than ever before. And now he was ready. Man and the claims of man no longer bound him.

Hunting their living meat, as the Yeehats were hunting it, on the flanks of the migrating moose, the wolf pack had at last crossed over from the land of streams and timber and invaded Buck's valley. Into the clearing where the moonlight streamed, they poured in a silvery flood; and in the center of the clearing stood Buck, waiting their coming. They were awed, so still and large he stood, and a moment's pause fell, till the boldest one leaped straight for him. Like a flash Buck struck, breaking the neck. Then he stood, without movement as before, the stricken wolf rolling in agony behind him. Three others tried it in sharp succession; and one after the other they drew back, streaming blood from throat or shoulders.

Then the whole pack flung forward, pell-mell, crowded together, blocked and confused by its eagerness to pull down the prey. Pivoting on his hind legs, snapping and gashing, Buck was everywhere at once, presenting a front which was apparently unbroken, so swiftly did he whirl and guard from side to side.

But to prevent them from getting behind him, he was forced back, down past the pool and into the creek bed, till he brought up against a high gravel bank. He worked along to a right angle in the bank, and here he came to bay, protected on three sides, with nothing to do but face the front.

And so well did he face it, that in half an hour the wolves drew back. The tongues of all were out and lolling, the white fangs showing cruelly white in the moonlight. Some lay down with heads raised and ears pricked forward; others stood watching him; some lapped water from the pool. One, long and lean and gray, advanced cautiously, and Buck recognized the wild brother with whom he had run for a night and a day. He was whining softly, and, as Buck whined, they touched noses.

Then an old wolf, gaunt and battle-scarred, came forward. Buck writhed his lips into a snarl, but sniffed noses with him. Whereupon the old wolf sat down, pointed nose at the moon, and broke out the long wolf howl. The others sat and howled. And now the call came to Buck in unmistakable accents. He, too, sat down and howled. This over, he came out of his angle and the pack crowded around him, sniffing in half-friendly, half-savage manner. The leaders lifted the yelp of the pack and sprang away into the woods. The wolves swung in behind. And Buck ran with them, beside the wild brother, yelping as he ran.

AND HERE MAY WELL END the story of Buck. The years were not many when the Yeehats noted a change in the breed of timber wolves; for some were seen with splashes of brown on head and muzzle, and with a rift of white centering down the chest. But more remarkable than this, the Yeehats tell of a Ghost Dog that runs at the head of the pack. They are afraid of this Ghost Dog, for it has cunning greater than they, stealing from their camps in fierce winters, robbing their traps, slaying their dogs, and defying their bravest hunters.

Nay, the tale grows worse. Hunters there are who fail to return to the camp, and hunters there have been whom their tribesmen found with throats slashed cruelly open and with wolf prints about them in the snow greater than the prints of any wolf. Each fall, when the Yeehats follow the moose, there is one valley which they never enter. And women there are who become sad when the word goes over the fire of how the Evil Spirit selected that valley for an abiding place.

In the summers there is one visitor, however, to that valley, of which the Yeehats do not know. It is a great, gloriously coated wolf, like, and yet unlike, all other wolves. He crosses alone from the smiling timberland and comes down into an open space among the trees. Here a yellow stream flows from rotted moosehide sacks and sinks into the ground, with long grasses growing through it and hiding its yellow from the sun; and here he muses for a time, howling once, long and mournfully, ere he departs.

But he is not always alone. When the long winter nights come on and the wolves follow their meat into the lower valleys, he may be seen running again at the head of the pack through the pale moonlight or glimmering borealis, leaping gigantic above his fellows, his great throat a-bellow as he sings a song of the younger world, which is the song of the pack.

Jack London
(1876–1916)

AUTHOR, SAILOR, REPORTER, treasure hunter, and social activist, Jack London was as adventurous as any fictional character he created. He was energetic and handsome, with gray-blue eyes and tousled blond hair. London drew on his extensive travels and experiences for inspiration. With his keen eye for detail and description and his discipline as a writer, London became one of the most prolific and popular writers of his day. His popularity has endured into our own time.

John Griffith London was born in Oakland, California, in 1876. His early years were spent in poverty. To escape the drudgery of his life, London turned to books and the sea, and both became lifelong loves. At fifteen, London scraped together enough money to buy a secondhand sailboat and joined the ranks of the "oyster pirates," colorful waterfront characters who raided commercial oyster beds in San Francisco Bay. Eventually, London moved to the right side of the law and joined the "fish patrol," the waterborne police force that protected the oyster beds from his former associates. At seventeen, London signed aboard a schooner and spent a year cruising the northern Pacific hunting seals for their highly prized pelts.

When London came home he could find only poor jobs and often no job at all. In 1894 he joined the ranks of "Kelley's Army," a group of unemployed men marching to Washington to demand jobs. London got as far as New York, where he was jailed for a month on a charge of vagrancy. He made his way back to the West Coast by riding the rails as a hobo. These experiences, and his wide reading of the socialist writers of the day, gave London a sense of social activism and concern for the underdog that lasted throughout his life.

In 1897 gold was discovered along the Klondike River in northwest Canada and Alaska. Hoping to strike it rich, London joined the hordes of men heading north in search of gold. He spent an adventurous year in the Klondike before sickness forced his return to California. He had failed to find gold, but his Klondike exploits proved to be a rich mother lode. In

December 1898 he sold his first story, a Klondike adventure called "To the Man on the Trail," for five dollars. By 1899 London's stories were being published regularly in national magazines. His first collection of short stories, *The Son of the Wolf*, was published in 1900. In 1903 *The Call of the Wild*, London's stirring story of a dog struggling to survive the rough climate and rougher men of the Klondike, became a best seller.

London used the profits from his writings to buy a thousand-acre ranch in Glen Ellen, California, and a sailboat, the *Snark*. He planned to take the *Snark* on a cruise around the world. With his wife and a few friends, he left San Francisco aboard the *Snark* in 1907. They made it across the Pacific before abandoning the expedition when London fell ill. As always, London turned his experiences into stories, publishing an account of the voyage, *The Cruise of the Snark*, and several stories set in the Pacific islands.

But his health declined and he struggled with a drinking problem. Despite his wealth—he was for a time the world's highest-paid writer—his lavish hospitality and the upkeep of his huge ranch brought him to the edge of bankruptcy. On November 22, 1916, London died in his beloved ranch house at Glen Ellen. No one knows for certain whether his death was caused by sickness or by an overdose of a pain-killing drug. He was forty years old.

Other Titles by Jack London

The Assassination Bureau, Ltd. New York: Penguin, 1978.

The Call of the Wild, White Fang, & Other Stories. Andrew Sinclair, editor. New York: Penguin, 1981.

The Cruise of the Dazzler. Oakland, CA: Star Rover, 1981.

The Cruise of the Snark. Wolfeboro, NH: Longwood, 1981.

Great Short Works of Jack London. Earle Labor, editor. New York: Harper & Row.

Jack London Stories. New York: Putnam, 1978.

The Man with the Gash. Oakland, CA: Star Rover, 1981.

Martin Eden. New York: Penguin, 1984.

The Sea Wolf. New York: Bantam, 1984.

To Build a Fire & Other Stories. New York: Bantam, 1986.

The Unabridged Jack London. Lawrence Teacher and Richard Nicholls, editors. Philadelphia: Running Press, 1981.

White Fang. New York: Scholastic, 1972.

Young Wolf: Early Adventure Stories of Jack London. San Bernardino, CA: Borgo Press, 1988.

Foreword

The hero of *Typhoon* is stolid, middle-aged Captain MacWhirr, of the steamer *Nan-Shan*, at first appearance a man totally lacking in heroic qualities. His first mate, Jukes, is by contrast young, talkative, and excitable. Off the China coast they are unexpectedly plunged into an inferno of wind and rain and roaring waves. How each reacts to the mighty storm, how each emerges from it, is the theme of this tautly written novella. Excitement blows with gale force through its pages, and the descriptive passages are of unsurpassed magnificence.

Joseph Conrad (1857–1924) is considered one of the great masters of English prose, although he grew up speaking only Polish. He was born in Poland and christened Teodor Jozef Konrad Korzeniowski. His parents died before he was ten years old. Though he had never seen the ocean, he felt its call at an early age, and at seventeen he made his way to Marseilles and got work on a French ship bound for South America. At twenty-one he joined the British merchant fleet, and he taught himself English so successfully that he became in time a naturalized citizen as well as a master mariner, commanding ships that plied the trade routes to Africa and the Orient.

Retiring from active service in 1893, Conrad settled in England, where he married and had two sons. He was now able to satisfy his growing desire to write in his adopted language, and the masterpieces that flowed from his pen include *Typhoon*, *Lord Jim*, *The Heart of Darkness*, *The Nigger of the Narcissus*, and *Youth*. Most of his work, like *Typhoon*, reflects his years as a sailor and dramatizes the plight of isolated men faced with momentous decisions.

TYPHOON

CHAPTER I

CAPTAIN MACWHIRR, OF THE STEAMER *Nan-Shan*, had a physiognomy that, in the order of material appearances, was the exact counterpart of his mind: it presented no marked characteristic of firmness or stupidity; it had no pronounced characteristics whatever; it was simply ordinary, irresponsive, and unruffled.

The only thing his aspect might have been said to suggest, at times, was bashfulness. He would sit, in business offices ashore, sunburnt and smiling faintly, with downcast eyes. When he raised them, they were perceived to be direct in their glance and of blue color. His hair was fair and extremely fine, clasping from temple to temple the bald dome of his skull in a clamp as of fluffy silk. The hair of his face, on the contrary, carroty and flaming, resembled a growth of copper wire; no matter how close he shaved, fiery metallic gleams passed, when he moved his head, over the surface of his cheeks. He was rather below the medium height, a bit round-shouldered, and so sturdy of limb that his clothes always looked a shade too tight for his arms and legs. He never left his ship for the shore without clutching in his powerful, hairy fist an elegant umbrella, generally unrolled. Young Jukes, the chief mate, attending his commander to the gangway, would sometimes venture to say, "Allow me, sir"—and possessing himself of the umbrella deferentially, would shake the folds, twirl a neat furl, and hand it back. Jukes would go through this performance with a face of such portentous gravity that Mr. Solomon Rout, the chief engineer, smoking his morning cigar over the skylight, would turn away to hide a smile. "Oh! Aye! . . . Thank 'ee, Jukes, thank 'ee," would mutter Captain MacWhirr, heartily, without looking up.

Having just enough imagination to carry him through each day, and no more, he was tranquilly sure of himself; and from the very same cause he was not in the least conceited. It is your imaginative officer who is touchy and difficult to please; but every ship Captain MacWhirr commanded was the floating abode of harmony and peace.

It was, in truth, impossible for him to take a flight of fancy. Yet the uninteresting lives of such men have their mysterious side. It was impossible in Captain MacWhirr's case, for instance, to understand what under heaven could have induced him, at the age of fifteen, to run away to sea. He had been the perfectly satisfactory son of a petty grocer in Belfast, and his father never really forgave him for this undutiful stupidity. "We could have got on without him," he used to say later on, "but there's the business. And he an only son, too!" His mother wept very much after his disappearance. As it had never occurred to him to leave word behind, he was mourned over for dead till, after eight months, his first letter arrived from Talcahuano. It was short, and contained the statement: "We had very fine weather on our passage out." The mother again wept copiously, while the remark, "Tom's an ass," expressed the emotions of the father.

MacWhirr's visits to his home were necessarily rare, and in the course of years he despatched other letters to his parents, informing them of his successive promotions and of his movements upon the vast earth. In these missives could be found sentences like this: "The heat here is very great." Or: "On Christmas day at 4 p.m. we fell in with some icebergs." The old people ultimately became acquainted with a good many names of ships, and with the names of the skippers who commanded them—with the names of seas, oceans, ports—with the names of islands—with the name of their son's young woman. She was called Lucy. It did not suggest itself to him to mention whether he thought the name pretty. And then they died.

The great day of MacWhirr's marriage came in due course, following shortly upon the great day when he got his first command.

All these events had taken place many years before the morning when, in the chart room of the steamer *Nan-Shan*, he stood confronted by the fall of a barometer he had no reason to distrust. The fall—taking into account the time of the year, and the ship's location—was ominous; but the red face of the man betrayed no inward disturbance. "That's a fall, and no mistake," he thought. "There must be some uncommonly dirty weather knocking about."

The *Nan-Shan* was on her way from the southward to the treaty port of Foochow, with some cargo in her lower holds, and two hundred Chinese coolies returning to their village homes after a few years of work in various tropical colonies. The morning was fine; the oily sea heaved without a sparkle. The foredeck, packed with Chinamen, was full of somber clothing, yellow faces, and pigtails, and sprinkled with a good many naked shoulders, for the heat was close. The coolies lounged, talked, smoked, or stared over the rail; some, drawing water over the side, sluiced each other; a few slept on hatches; and every single one of them was carrying with him all he had in the world—a wooden chest with brass on the corners, containing the savings of his labors: some clothes of ceremony, sticks of incense, a little opium maybe, bits of nameless rubbish, and a small hoard of silver dollars—toiled for in coal lighters, grubbed out of earth, sweated out in mines, amassed patiently, guarded with care, cherished fiercely.

A cross swell had set in about ten o'clock, without disturbing these passengers much, because the *Nan-Shan*, with her great breadth of beam, was an exceptionally steady ship. Mr. Jukes, in moments of expansion on shore, would proclaim loudly that the "old girl was as good as she was pretty." It would never have occurred to Captain MacWhirr to express his opinion in terms so fanciful.

She was a good ship, undoubtedly, and not old either. She had been built in Dumbarton less than three years before, to the order of a firm of merchants in Siam—Messrs. Sigg and Son. When she lay afloat, finished in every detail, the builders contemplated her with pride.

"Sigg has asked us for a reliable skipper," remarked one of the partners; and the other, reflecting, said: "I think MacWhirr is ashore at present." "Is he? Then wire him. He's the very man," declared the senior, without a moment's hesitation.

Next morning MacWhirr stood before them, having traveled from London by the midnight express. The three men started to view the *Nan-Shan* from stem to stern. Captain MacWhirr began by taking off his coat, which he hung on the end of a steam windlass embodying all the latest improvements.

"My uncle has written favorably of you to our good friends— Messrs. Sigg, you know—and doubtless they'll continue you out there in command," said the junior partner. "You'll be in charge of the handiest boat of her size on the coast of China, Captain."

"Have you? Thank 'ee," mumbled vaguely MacWhirr, to whom the view of a distant eventuality could make no appeal; and his eyes happening to be at rest upon the lock of the cabin door, he walked up to it and rattled the handle vigorously, while he observed, in his earnest voice, "You can't trust the workmen nowadays. A brand-new lock, and it won't act at all. Stuck fast. See?"

As soon as they found themselves alone in their office: "You praised that fellow up to Sigg. What is it you see in him?" asked the nephew, with faint contempt.

"I admit he has nothing of your fancy skipper about him, if that's what you mean," said the elder man, curtly. "Is the foreman of the joiners on the *Nan-Shan* outside? . . . Come in, Bates. How is it that you let Tait's people put a defective lock on the cabin door? The Captain could see directly he set eye on it. Have it replaced at once. . . ."

The lock was replaced accordingly, and a few days afterwards the *Nan-Shan* steamed out to the East, without MacWhirr having offered any further remark as to her fittings, or having been heard to utter a single word hinting at pride in his ship or gratitude for his appointment. Indeed he found very little occasion to talk.

JACK LONDON

(Handcoloring by Simon Hu)

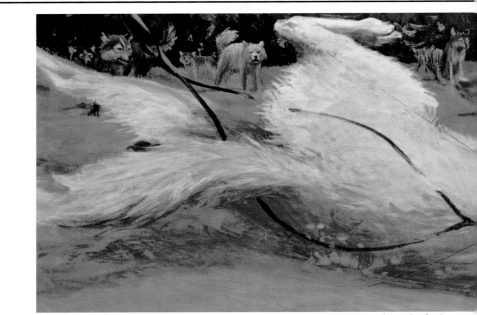

Thrice Buck tried to knock him over, then repeated the trick and broke the right foreleg.

The overloaded sled forged ahead, Buck and his mates struggling frantically under the rain of blows.

TYPHOON

With a tearing crash and a swirling, raving tumult, tons of water fell upon the deck, as though the ship had darted under the foot of a cataract.

On a bright sunshiny day, with the breeze chasing her smoke, the Nan-Shan*
came into Foochow.*

There were matters of duty, of course—orders, and so on; but the past being to his mind done with, and the future not there yet, the more general actualities of the day required no comment—because facts can speak for themselves with overwhelming precision.

Old Mr. Sigg liked a man of few words, and one that "you could be sure would not try to improve upon his instructions." Mac-Whirr, satisfying these requirements, was continued in command of the *Nan-Shan*, and applied himself to the careful navigation of his ship in the China seas. She had come out on a British register, but after some time Messrs. Sigg judged it expedient to transfer her to the Siamese flag.

At the news of the contemplated transfer young Jukes grew restless, as if personally affronted. He went about grumbling. "Fancy having a ridiculous Noah's Ark elephant in the ensign of one's ship," he said once at the engine-room door. "Dash me if I can stand it: I'll throw up the billet. Don't it make *you* sick, Mr. Rout?" he said to the chief engineer. But the chief engineer only cleared his throat with the air of a man who knows the value of a good billet.

The first morning the new flag floated over the stern of the *Nan-Shan* Jukes stood looking at it bitterly from the bridge. He struggled with his feelings for a while, and then remarked, "Queer flag for a man to sail under, sir."

"What's the matter with the flag?" inquired Captain MacWhirr. "Seems all right to me." And he walked across the bridge to have a good look.

"Well, it looks queer to me," burst out Jukes, exasperated, and flung off the bridge.

Captain MacWhirr was amazed at these manners. After a while he stepped into the chart room, and opened his Signal Code book to where the flags of all nations are figured in gaudy rows. He ran his finger over them, and when he came to Siam he contemplated with great attention the red field and the white elephant; and to make sure he brought the book out on the bridge to compare the colored drawing with the real thing at the flagstaff. When next Jukes happened on the bridge, his commander observed:

"There's nothing amiss with that flag."

"Isn't there?" mumbled Jukes.

"No. I looked up the book. Length twice the breadth and the elephant exactly in the middle. I thought the people ashore would know how to make the local flag. Stands to reason. You were wrong, Jukes. . . ."

"Well, sir," began Jukes, excitedly, "all I can say—"

"That's all right." Captain MacWhirr soothed him, sitting heavily on a little canvas folding stool he greatly affected. "All you have to do is to take care they don't hoist the elephant upside down before they get quite used to it. Because it would be, I suppose, understood as a signal of distress," he went on. "What do you think? That elephant there, I take it, stands for something in the nature of the Union Jack in the flag. . . ."

"Does it!" yelled Jukes, so that every head on deck looked towards the bridge. Then he sighed, and with sudden resignation: "It would certainly be a dam' distressful sight," he said, meekly.

Later in the day he accosted the chief engineer. "Here, let me tell you the old man's latest."

Mr. Solomon Rout (frequently alluded to as Long Sol, Old Sol, or Father Rout) found himself almost invariably the tallest man on board every ship he joined. His hair was scant and sandy, his flat cheeks were pale, and his bony wrists and long scholarly hands were pale, too. He smiled from on high at Jukes in the manner of a kind uncle lending an ear to the tale of an excited schoolboy. Then, greatly amused but impassive, he asked:

"And did you throw up the billet?"

"No," cried Jukes, raising a discouraged voice above the harsh buzz of the *Nan-Shan*'s friction winches. All of them were hard at work, loading cargo. "No, I didn't. What's the good? I might just as well fling my resignation at this bulkhead. I don't believe you can make a man like that understand anything."

At that moment Captain MacWhirr, back from the shore, crossed the deck, umbrella in hand, escorted by a mournful, self-possessed Chinaman, who walked behind him also carrying an umbrella.

The master of the *Nan-Shan*, speaking just audibly and gazing at his boots as his manner was, remarked that it would be necessary to call at Foochow this trip, and desired Mr. Rout to have steam up tomorrow afternoon at one o'clock sharp. Then Jukes was directed in the same subdued voice to keep the forward tween-deck clear of cargo. Two hundred coolies were going to be put down there. The Bun Hin Company were sending them home. Twenty-five bags of rice would be coming off in a sampan directly, for stores. All seven-years'-men they were, said Captain MacWhirr, with a camphorwood chest to every man. The carpenter should be set to work nailing three-inch battens along the deck below, to keep these boxes from shifting in a seaway. This Chinaman here was coming with the ship as far as Foochow—he would be a sort of interpreter. Bun Hin's clerk he was, and wanted to have a look at the space. Jukes had better take him forward. "D'ye hear, Jukes?"

Jukes had punctuated these instructions in the proper places with the obligatory "Yes, sir." His brusque "Come along, John; make look see" set the Chinaman in motion at his heels. Having no talent for foreign languages, Jukes mangled the very pidgin English cruelly. He pointed at the open hatch. "Catchee number one piecie place to sleep in. Eh?"

He was gruff, but not unfriendly. The Chinaman, gazing sad and speechless into the darkness of the hatchway, seemed to stand at the head of a yawning grave.

"No catchee rain down there—savee?" pointed out Jukes. "Suppose all'ee same fine weather, coolieman come topside," he pursued. "Savee, John?"

The Chinaman, who concealed his distrust under a gentle and refined melancholy, glanced out of his almond eyes from Jukes to the hatch and back again. "Velly good," he murmured, in a disconsolate undertone. Hastening smoothly away along the decks, he disappeared, ducking low under a sling of gunny-bags full of some costly merchandise and exhaling a repulsive smell.

Captain MacWhirr meantime had gone on the bridge and into the chart room, where a letter, commenced two days before, awaited termination. These long letters began with the words, "My darling wife," and the steward, between the scrubbing of the floors and the dusting of chronometer boxes, snatched at every opportunity to read them. They interested him much more than they possibly could the woman for whose eye they were intended; and this for the reason that they related in minute detail each successive trip of the *Nan-Shan*.

Her master, faithful to facts, which alone his consciousness reflected, would set them down with painstaking care upon many pages. The house in a northern suburb of London to which these pages were addressed had a bit of garden before the bow windows and colored glass with imitation lead frame in the front door. He paid forty pounds a year for it, and did not think the rent too high, because Mrs. MacWhirr (a pretentious person with a scraggy neck and a disdainful manner) was admittedly ladylike, and in the neighborhood was considered as "quite superior." The only secret of her life was her abject terror of the time when her husband would come home to stay. Under the same roof there dwelt also a daughter called Lydia and a son, Tom. These two were but slightly acquainted with their father. They knew him as a rare but privileged visitor, who smoked his pipe in the dining room and slept in the house. The lanky girl was rather ashamed of him; the boy was frankly and utterly indifferent.

And Captain MacWhirr wrote home from the coast of China twelve times every year, desiring quaintly to be "remembered to the children," and calmly subscribing himself "your loving husband."

The China Seas north and south are narrow seas. They are full of everyday, eloquent facts, such as islands, sandbanks, reefs— facts that speak to a seaman in clear, definite language. Their speech appealed to Captain MacWhirr so forcibly that he had given up his stateroom and practically lived on the bridge of his ship, sleeping at night in the chart room. And he indited there his home letters. Each of them, without exception, contained the phrase, "The weather has been very fine this trip," or some other statement to that effect. And this statement, too, was of the same perfect accuracy as all the others the letters contained.

Mr. Rout likewise wrote letters; only no one on board knew how chatty he could be pen in hand, because the chief engineer had enough imagination to keep his desk locked. His wife relished his style greatly. They were a childless couple, and Mrs. Rout, a big, high-bosomed, jolly woman of forty, shared with Mr. Rout's toothless and venerable mother a little cottage near Teddington. She would run over her correspondence, at breakfast, with lively eyes, and scream out passages in a joyous voice at the deaf old lady, prefacing each extract by the warning shout, "Solomon says!" She had the trick of firing off Solomon's utterances also upon strangers, astonishing them by the unfamiliar text and the jocular vein of these quotations. On the day when the new curate called for the first time, she found occasion to remark, "As Solomon says: 'The engineers that go down to the sea in ships behold the wonders of sailor nature.'" A change in the visitor's countenance made her stop and stare.

"Solomon . . . Oh! . . . Mrs. Rout," stuttered the young man. "I must say . . . I don't . . ."

"He's my husband," she announced in a great shout. Perceiving the joke, she laughed immoderately with a handkerchief to her eyes, while he sat wearing a forced smile, fully persuaded that she must be insane. They became excellent friends afterwards, and he learned in time to receive without flinching further scraps of Solomon's wisdom.

On the other hand, Mr. Jukes, unmarried, was in the habit of opening his heart to an old chum and former shipmate who served as second officer on board an Atlantic liner.

First of all he would insist upon the advantages of the Eastern trade, hinting at its superiority to the Western ocean service. He extolled the sky, the seas, and the ships of the Far East. The *Nan-Shan*, he affirmed, was second to none as a sea boat.

"We have no brassbound uniforms, but then we are like brothers here," he wrote. "We all mess together and live like fighting cocks. . . . All the chaps of the black squad are as decent as they make that kind, and Old Sol, the Chief, is a dry stick. We are good friends. As to our old man, you could not find a quieter skipper. Sometimes you would think he hadn't sense enough to see anything wrong. And yet it isn't that. Can't be. He doesn't do anything actually foolish, and gets his ship along all right without worrying anybody. Old Sol says he hasn't much conversation. Conversation! Lord! He never talks. The other day I had been yarning under the bridge with one of the engineers, and he must have heard us. When I came up to take my watch, he steps out of the chart room, and by and by he says: 'Was that you talking just now with the third engineer?' 'Yes, sir.' He walks off to starboard, and for half an hour perhaps he makes no sound. Then he strolls back to where I was. 'I can't understand what you can find to talk about,' says he. 'Two solid hours. I am not blaming you. I see people ashore at it all day long, and then in the evening they keep at it over drinks. Must be saying the same things over and over again. I can't understand.'

"Did you ever hear anything like that? And he was so patient about it. It made me quite sorry for him. But he is exasperating, too, sometimes. Of course one would not do anything to vex him even if it were worthwhile. But it isn't. He's too dense to trouble about, and that's the truth."

Thus wrote Mr. Jukes, out of the fullness of his heart, to his chum in the Western ocean.

He had expressed his honest opinion. It was not worthwhile trying to impress a man like MacWhirr.

He was not alone in his opinion. The sea itself, as if sharing Mr. Jukes' good-natured forbearance, had never put itself out to startle the silent man, who seldom looked up, and wandered innocently over its waters. Dirty weather MacWhirr had known, of course. He had been made wet, uncomfortable, tired in the usual way, felt at the time and presently forgotten. So that upon the whole he had been justified in reporting fine weather at home. But he had never been given a glimpse of immeasurable strength and of immoderate wrath, the wrath that passes exhausted but never appeased—the wrath and fury of the passionate sea. He knew it existed, as we know that crime and abominations exist; he had heard of it as a peaceable citizen hears of battles, famines, and floods, and yet knows nothing of what these things mean. Captain MacWhirr had sailed over the surface of the oceans as some men go skimming over the years of existence, to sink gently into a placid grave, ignorant of life to the last, without ever having been made to see all it may contain of perfidy, of violence, and of terror. There are on sea and land such men thus fortunate—or thus disdained by destiny or by the sea.

CHAPTER II

OBSERVING THE STEADY FALL of the barometer, Captain MacWhirr thought, "There's some dirty weather knocking about."

This is precisely what he thought. He had had experience of moderately dirty weather—the term dirty as applied to the weather implying only moderate discomfort to the seaman. Had he been informed by an indisputable authority that the end of the world was to be accomplished by a catastrophic disturbance of the atmosphere, he would have assimilated the information under the simple idea of dirty weather, and no other, because he had had no experience of cataclysms.

The wisdom of his country had pronounced by an Act of Parliament that before he could be considered fit to take charge of a ship he should be able to answer certain questions on the subject of circular storms such as hurricanes, cyclones, typhoons; and apparently he had answered them, since he was now in command of the *Nan-Shan*. But if he had answered he remembered nothing of it. He was, however, conscious of being made uncomfortable by the clammy heat. He came out on the bridge, and found no relief to this oppression. He gasped like a fish, and began to believe himself greatly out of sorts.

The *Nan-Shan* was plowing a vanishing furrow upon the circle of the sea that had the surface and the shimmer of an undulating piece of gray silk. The sun, pale and without rays, poured down leaden heat in a strangely indecisive light, and the Chinamen were lying prostrate about the decks. Their bloodless, pinched, yellow faces were like the faces of bilious invalids. Three of them away forward were quarreling barbarously; and one big fellow, half naked, with Herculean shoulders, was hanging limply over a winch; another, sitting on the deck, his knees up and his head drooping sideways in a girlish attitude, was plaiting his pigtail with infinite languor. The smoke struggled with difficulty out of the funnel, and instead of streaming away spread itself out like an infernal sort of cloud, raining soot all over the decks.

"What the devil are you doing there, Mr. Jukes?" asked Captain MacWhirr.

This unusual form of address, though mumbled rather than spoken, caused Mr. Jukes to start as though he had been prodded under the fifth rib. He was sitting on a low bench with a piece of canvas stretched over his knees, pushing a sail needle vigorously. He looked up, and surprise gave his eyes an expression of inno-cence and candor.

"I am only roping some of that new set of bags we made last trip for whipping up coals," he remonstrated, gently. "We shall want them for the next coaling, sir."

"What became of the others?"

"Why, worn out of course, sir."

Captain MacWhirr, glaring down irresolutely, disclosed the gloomy conviction that more than half of them had been lost overboard, "if only the truth was known," and retired to the other end of the bridge. Jukes, exasperated by this unprovoked attack, broke the needle, and getting up he cursed the heat in a violent undertone.

The propeller thumped, the three Chinamen forward suddenly gave up squabbling, and the one who had been plaiting his tail clasped his legs and stared dejectedly over his knees. The lurid sunshine cast faint and sickly shadows. The swell ran higher and swifter every moment, and the ship lurched heavily in the deep hollows of the sea.

"I wonder where that beastly swell comes from," said Jukes aloud, recovering himself after a stagger.

"Northeast," grunted the literal MacWhirr, from his side of the bridge. "There's some dirty weather knocking about. Go and look at the glass."

When Jukes came out of the chart room, the cast of his countenance had changed to thoughtfulness and concern. He caught
hold of the bridge rail and stared ahead.

The temperature in the engine room had gone up to a hundred
and seventeen degrees. Irritated voices were ascending through
the skylight and through the fiddle of the stokehold in a harsh and
resonant uproar, mingled with angry clangs and scrapes of metal,
as if men with limbs of iron and throats of bronze had been quarreling down there. The second engineer was falling foul of the
stokers for letting the steam go down. The stokers were answering
him back restlessly, slamming the furnace doors with the fury of
despair. Then the noise ceased suddenly, and the second engineer
appeared, emerging out of the stokehold streaked with grime
and soaking wet.

As soon as his head was clear of the fiddle he began to scold
Jukes for not trimming properly the stokehold ventilators. In
answer Jukes made with his hands deprecatory soothing signs
meaning: "No wind—can't be helped—you can see for yourself."
But the other wouldn't hear reason. His teeth flashed angrily in
his dirty face. He didn't mind, he said, the trouble of punching
their blanked heads down there, blank his soul, but did the con-
demned sailors think you could keep steam up in the godforsaken
boilers simply by knocking the blanked stokers about? No, by
George! You had to get some draft, too—and what did Jukes think
he was stuck up there for, if he couldn't get one of his decayed,
good-for-nothing deck cripples to turn the ventilators to the wind?

The relations of the "engine room" and the "deck" of the *Nan-
Shan* were, as is known, of a brotherly nature; therefore Jukes
begged the other in a restrained tone not to make a disgusting ass
of himself; the skipper was on the other side of the bridge. But
the second declared mutinously that he didn't care a rap who was
on the other side of the bridge. Jukes, at that, invited him in
unflattering terms to come up and twist the beastly things to please
himself, and catch such wind as a donkey of his sort could find. The
second rushed up to the fray and flung himself at the port ventilator. All he did was to move the cowl round a few inches, and

seemed spent in the effort. He leaned against the wheelhouse, and Jukes walked up to him.

"Oh, heavens!" ejaculated the engineer in a feeble voice. He lifted his eyes to the sky. "Heavens! Phew! What's up, anyhow?"

Jukes, straddling his long legs like a pair of compasses, put on an air of superiority. "We're going to catch it this time," he said. "The barometer is tumbling down like anything, Harry. And you trying to kick up that silly row. . . ."

The word "barometer" seemed to revive the second engineer's animosity. Collecting afresh all his energies, he directed Jukes in a low and brutal tone to shove the unmentionable instrument down his gory throat, and dashed off. He stopped upon the fiddle long enough to shake his fist at the unnatural daylight, and dropped into the dark hole with a whoop.

When Jukes turned, his eyes fell upon Captain MacWhirr. MacWhirr did not look at his chief officer, but said at once, "That's a very violent man, that second engineer."

"Jolly good second, anyhow," grunted Jukes. "They can't keep up steam," he added, rapidly, and made a grab at the rail against a coming lurch.

Captain MacWhirr, unprepared, took a run and brought himself up with a jerk by an awning stanchion.

"A profane man," he said, obstinately. "If this goes on, I'll have to get rid of him."

"It's the heat," said Jukes. "The weather's awful. It would make a saint swear. Even up here I feel exactly as if I had my head tied up in a blanket."

Captain MacWhirr looked up. "D'ye mean to say, Mr. Jukes, you ever had your head tied up in a blanket? What was that for?"

"It's a manner of speaking, sir," said Jukes, stolidly.

"Some of you fellows do go on! What's that about saints swearing? What sort of saint would that be that would swear? . . . The heat does not make me swear—does it? It's filthy bad temper. That's what it is."

And Jukes, incorrigible, thought, "Goodness me! Somebody's put a new inside to my old man. Here's temper, if you like. Of course it's the weather; what else? It would make an angel quarrelsome—let alone a saint."

All the Chinamen on deck appeared at their last gasp.

At its setting the sun had a diminished diameter and an expiring brown, rayless glow. A dense bank of cloud became visible to the northward; it had a sinister dark olive tint, and lay low and motionless upon the sea, resembling a solid obstacle in the path of the ship. She went floundering towards it like an exhausted creature driven to its death. The coppery twilight retired slowly, and the darkness brought out overhead a swarm of unsteady, big stars, that seemed to hang very near the earth. At eight o'clock Jukes went into the chart room to write up the ship's log.

He copied neatly out of the rough book the number of miles, the course of the ship, and in the column for WIND scrawled the word "Calm" from top to bottom of the eight hours since noon. He was exasperated by the continuous, monotonous rolling of the ship. The heavy inkstand slid away in a manner that suggested perverse intelligence in dodging the pen. Having written in the space under REMARKS "Heat very oppressive," he stuck the end of the penholder in his teeth and mopped his face.

"Ship rolling heavily in a high cross swell," he began again, and commented to himself, "Heavily is no word for it." Then, sprawling over the table with arrested pen, he glanced out of the door, and in that frame of his vision he saw all the stars flying upwards between the teakwood jambs on a black sky. The whole lot took flight together and disappeared, leaving only the blackness of the sea flecked with white flashes of foam. The stars that had flown to the roll came back on the return swing of the ship, rushing downwards in their glittering multitude, not of fiery points, but enlarged to tiny disks brilliant with a clear wet sheen.

Jukes watched the flying big stars for a moment, and then wrote: "8 p.m. Swell increasing. Ship laboring. Battened down the coolies for the night. Barometer still falling." He paused, and thought to himself, "Perhaps nothing whatever'll come of it." And then he closed resolutely his entries: "Every appearance of a typhoon coming on."

On going out he had to stand aside, and Captain MacWhirr strode over the doorstep without saying a word or making a sign. It was Jukes' watch below, but he yearned for communion with his kind; and out on the bridge he remarked cheerily to the second mate, "Doesn't look so bad, after all—does it?"

The second mate, managing with difficulty the shifting slope of the deck, made no reply. "Hallo! That's a heavy one," said Jukes, swaying to meet the long roll till his lowered hand touched the planks. This time the second mate made in his throat a noise of an unfriendly nature.

He was an oldish, shabby little fellow, with bad teeth and no hair on his face. He had been shipped in a hurry in Shanghai, one trip when the second officer brought from home had contrived (in some manner Captain MacWhirr could never understand) to fall overboard into an empty coal lighter lying alongside, and had to be sent to the hospital with concussion and a broken limb or two.

Jukes was not discouraged by the unsympathetic sound. "The Chinamen must be having a lovely time of it down there," he said. "It's lucky for them the old girl has an easy roll. There now! This one wasn't so bad."

"You wait," snarled the second mate.

With his sharp nose, red at the tip, and his thin pinched lips, he always looked as though he were raging inwardly. All his time off duty he spent in his cabin with the door shut, keeping so still in there that he was supposed to be asleep; but the man who came in to wake him for his watch on deck would invariably find him in the bunk with his eyes wide open, and glaring irritably from a soiled pillow. He was one of those men who are picked up at need in the ports of the world. They are competent enough, show no evidence of any sort of vice, and carry about them all the signs of manifest failure. They come aboard on an emergency, care for no ship afloat, and make up their minds to leave at inconvenient times. They clear out with no words of leave-taking in some god-forsaken port other men would fear to be stranded in, and go ashore in company of a shabby sea chest, corded like a treasure box, and with an air of shaking the ship's dust off their feet.

"You wait," he repeated, with his back to Jukes, motionless and implacable.

"Do you mean to say we are going to catch it hot?" asked Jukes with boyish interest.

"Say? . . . I say nothing. You don't catch me," snapped the little second mate, with a mixture of pride, scorn, and cunning, as if Jukes' question had been a trap. "Oh, no! None of you here shall make a fool of me if I know it," he mumbled to himself.

Jukes reflected rapidly that this second mate was a mean little beast, and in his heart he wished poor Jack Allen had never smashed himself up in the coal lighter. The far-off blackness ahead of the ship was like another night seen through the starry night of the earth—the starless night of immensities beyond the created universe.

"Whatever there might be about," said Jukes, "we are steaming straight into it."

"*You've* said it," caught up the second mate. "You've said it, mind—not I."

"Oh, go to Jericho!" said Jukes, frankly; and the other emitted a triumphant little chuckle.

The ship, after a pause of comparative steadiness, now started upon a series of rolls, one worse than the other, and for a time Jukes, preserving his equilibrium, was too busy to open his mouth. As soon as the violent swinging had quieted down somewhat, he said, "This is a bit too much of a good thing. Whether anything is coming or not I think she ought to be put head on to that swell. The old man is just gone in to lie down. Hang me if I don't speak to him."

When he opened the door of the chart room he saw his captain reading a book. Captain MacWhirr was standing up with one hand grasping the edge of the bookshelf and the other holding open before his face a thick volume. The lamp wriggled in the gimbals, the long barometer swung in jerky circles, and the table altered its slant every moment. In the midst of all this movement Captain MacWhirr, holding on, showed his eyes above the upper edge, and asked, "What's the matter?"

"Swell getting worse, sir."

"Noticed that in here," muttered Captain MacWhirr. "Anything wrong?"

Jukes, inwardly disconcerted by the seriousness of the eyes looking at him over the top of the book, produced an embarrassed grin.

"Rolling like old boots," he said, sheepishly.

"Aye! Very heavy—very heavy. What do you want?"

At this Jukes lost his footing and began to flounder.

"I was thinking of our passengers," he said, like a man clutching at a straw.

"Passengers?" wondered the Captain, gravely.

"Why, the Chinamen, sir," explained Jukes, very sick of this conversation.

"The Chinamen! Why don't you speak plainly? Never heard of a lot of coolies spoken of as passengers before. What's come to you?" Captain MacWhirr, closing the book on his forefinger, looked completely mystified. "Why are you thinking of the Chinamen, Mr. Jukes?" he inquired.

Jukes took a plunge, like a man driven to it. "She's rolling her decks full of water, sir. Thought you might put her head on perhaps—for a while—till this goes down a bit. Head to the eastward."

He held on in the doorway, and Captain MacWhirr, feeling his grip on the shelf inadequate, made up his mind to let go in a hurry, and fell heavily on the couch.

"Head to the eastward?" he said, struggling to sit up. "That's more than four points off her course."

"Yes, sir. Would just bring her head round enough to meet this. . . ."

Captain MacWhirr was now sitting up. He had not dropped the book. "To the eastward?" he repeated, with dawning astonishment. "To the . . . Where do you think we are bound to? You want me to haul a full-powered steamship four points off her course to make the Chinamen comfortable! Now, I've heard more than enough of mad things done in the world—but this . . . Why, there's no wind—it's a dead calm, isn't it, Jukes?"

"It is, sir. But there's something out of the common coming, for sure."

"Maybe. I suppose you have a notion I should be getting out of the way of that dirt," said Captain MacWhirr, fixing the oilcloth on the floor with a heavy stare. Thus he noticed neither Jukes' discomfiture nor the mixture of vexation and astonished respect on his face.

"Now, here's this book," he continued with deliberation, slapping his thigh with the volume. "I've been reading the chapter on the storms there."

This was true. He had been reading the chapter on the storms. When he had entered the chart room, some influence in the air—the same influence, probably, that had caused the steward to bring without orders the Captain's seaboots and oilskin coat up to the chart room—had as it were guided his hand to the shelf; and without taking the time to sit down he had waded into the subject. He lost himself amongst advancing semicircles, left- and right-hand quadrants, the probable bearing of the center, the shifts of the wind and the readings of barometer. He tried to bring all these things into a definite relation to himself, and ended by becoming contemptuously angry with such a lot of words, all headwork and supposition, without a glimmer of certitude.

"It's the damnedest thing, Jukes," he said. "If a fellow was to believe all that's in there, he would be running most of his time all over the sea trying to get behind the weather."

Jukes opened his mouth, but said nothing.

"Running to get behind the weather! Do you understand that, Mr. Jukes? It's the maddest thing!" ejaculated Captain MacWhirr, with pauses. "You would think an old woman had been writing this. It passes me. If that thing means anything useful, then it means that I should at once alter the course away, away to the devil somewhere, and come booming down on Foochow from the northward at the tail of this dirty weather that's supposed to be knocking about in our way. From the north! Do you understand, Mr. Jukes? Three hundred extra miles to the distance, and a pretty coal bill to show. I couldn't bring myself to do that if every word in there was gospel truth, Mr. Jukes. Don't you expect me . . ."

And Jukes, silent, marveled at this display of feeling and loquacity.

"But the truth is that you don't know if the fellow is right, anyhow. How can you tell what a gale is made of till you get it? Very well. Here he says that the center of them things bears eight points off the wind; but we haven't got any wind, for all the barometer falling. Where's his center now?"

"We will get the wind presently," mumbled Jukes.

"Let it come, then," said Captain MacWhirr, with dignified indignation. "It's only to let you see, Mr. Jukes, that you don't find everything in books. All these rules for dodging breezes, Mr. Jukes, seem to me the maddest thing, when you come to look at it sensibly."

He raised his eyes, and saw Jukes gazing at him dubiously.

"About as queer as your extraordinary notion of dodging the ship head to sea, to make the Chinamen comfortable; whereas all we've got to do is to take them to Foochow, being timed to get there before noon on Friday. If the weather delays me—very well. But suppose I went swinging off my course and came in two days late, and they asked me: 'Where have you been all that time, Captain?' What could I say to that? 'Went around to dodge the bad weather,' I would say. 'It must've been dam' bad,' they would say. 'Don't know,' I would have to say; 'I've dodged clear of it.' See that, Jukes? I have been thinking it all out this afternoon."

He looked up again in his unseeing, unimaginative way. No one had ever heard him say so much at one time. Jukes, with his arms open in the doorway, was like a man beholding a miracle. Unbounded wonder was in his eye.

"A gale is a gale, Mr. Jukes," resumed the Captain, "and a full-powered steamship has got to face it. There's just so much dirty weather knocking about the world, and the proper thing is to go through it—with none of what old Captain Wilson of the *Melita* calls 'storm strategy.' The other day ashore I heard him hold forth about it to a lot of shipmasters who sat at a table next to mine. It seemed to me the greatest nonsense. He was telling them how he outmaneuvered, I think he said, a terrific gale, so that it never came nearer than fifty miles. A neat piece of headwork he called it. How he knew there was a terrific gale fifty miles off beats me altogether. It was like listening to a crazy man. I would have thought Captain Wilson old enough to know better."

Captain MacWhirr ceased for a moment, then said, "It's your watch below, Mr. Jukes?"

Jukes came to himself with a start. "Yes, sir."

"Leave orders to call me at the slightest change," said the Captain. He put the book away, and tucked his legs upon the couch. "Shut the door so that it don't fly open, will you? I can't stand a door banging. They've put a lot of rubbishy locks into this ship, I must say."

Captain MacWhirr closed his eyes.

He did so to rest himself. He was tired, and he experienced that state of mental vacuity which comes at the end of an exhaustive discussion that has liberated some belief matured in the course of meditative years. He had indeed been making his confession of faith, had he only known it; and its effect was to make Jukes, on the other side of the door, stand scratching his head for a good while.

Captain MacWhirr opened his eyes.

He thought he must have been asleep. What was that loud noise? Wind? Why had he not been called? The lamp wriggled in its gimbals, the barometer swung in circles, a pair of limp seaboots with collapsed tops went sliding past the couch. He put out his hand and captured one. Jukes' face appeared in a crack of the door. A piece of paper flew up, a rush of air enveloped Captain Mac-Whirr. Beginning to draw on the boot, he gazed at Jukes' excited features.

"Came on like this," shouted Jukes, "five minutes ago . . . all of a sudden."

The head disappeared with a bang, and a heavy splash and patter of drops swept past the closed door as if a pailful of melted lead had been flung against the house. A whistling could be heard now, outside, and the stuffy chart room seemed as full of drafts as a shed. Captain MacWhirr collared the other seaboot on its violent passage along the floor. He was not flustered, but he could not find at once the opening for his foot. The shoes he had flung off were scurrying from end to end of the cabin, gamboling playfully over each other like puppies. As soon as he stood up he kicked at them viciously, but without effect.

He threw himself into the attitude of a lunging fencer to reach his oilskin coat; and afterwards he staggered all over the confined space while he jerked himself into it. Straddling his legs far apart, and with a strained, listening attention, he tied the strings of his sou'wester under his chin, with thick fingers that trembled slightly. The confused clamor that had beset his ship filled his ears; it was tumultuous and very loud—made up of the rush of the wind, the crashes of the sea, and that prolonged deep vibration of the air which is like the roll of an immense and remote drum. Once dressed, he stood for a moment in the light of the lamp, thick, clumsy, shapeless in his panoply of combat, vigilant and red-faced.

"There's a lot of weight in this," he muttered.

As soon as he attempted to open the door the wind caught it. Clinging to the handle, he was dragged out over the doorstep, and at once found himself engaged with the wind in a sort of personal scuffle whose object was the shutting of that door. At the last moment a tongue of air scurried in and licked out the flame of the lamp.

Ahead of the ship he perceived a great darkness lying upon a multitude of white flashes; on the starboard beam a few amazing stars drooped, dim and fitful, above an immense waste of broken seas, as if seen through a mad drift of smoke.

On the bridge a knot of men, indistinct, were making great efforts in the light of the wheelhouse windows. Suddenly darkness closed upon one pane, then on another. The voices of the group reached him in shreds and fragments of forlorn shouting snatched past the ear. All at once Jukes appeared at his side, yelling, with his head down.

"Watch—put in—wheelhouse shutters—glass—afraid—blow in."

Jukes heard his commander upbraiding. "This—come—warning—call me." He tried to explain, but the uproar pressed on his lips. Then they gained the shelter of the weather cloth, and could converse with raised voices, as people quarrel.

"I got the hands to cover up the ventilators. Good job I had remained on deck. I didn't think you would be asleep, and so . . . What did you say, sir? What?"

"Nothing," cried Captain MacWhirr. "I said—all right. You haven't altered her course?"

"No, sir. Certainly not. Wind came out right ahead. And here comes the head sea."

A plunge of the ship ended in a shock as if she had landed her forefoot upon something solid. After a moment of stillness a lofty flight of sprays drove hard upon their faces.

"Keep her at it as long as we can," shouted Captain MacWhirr.

Before Jukes had squeezed the salt water out of his eyes all the stars had disappeared.

CHAPTER III

JUKES WAS AS READY a man as any half-dozen young mates that may be caught by casting a net upon the waters; and though he had been somewhat taken aback by the startling viciousness of the first squall, he had pulled himself together on the instant, had called out the hands and had rushed them along to secure such openings about the deck as had not been battened down earlier in the evening. Shouting, "Jump, boys, and bear a hand!" he led in the work, telling himself the while that he had "just expected this."

But at the same time he was growing aware that this was rather more than he had expected. From the first stir of the air felt on his cheek the gale seemed to take upon itself the accumulated impetus of an avalanche. Heavy sprays enveloped the *Nan-Shan* from stem to stern, and in the midst of her regular rolling she began to jerk and plunge as though she had gone mad with fright.

Jukes thought, "This is no joke." While he was exchanging explanatory yells with his captain, a sudden lowering of the darkness came upon the night, falling before their vision like something palpable. It was as if the masked lights of the world had been turned down. Jukes was uncritically glad to have his captain at hand. It relieved him as though that man had, by simply coming on deck, taken most of the gale's weight upon his shoulders. Such is the prestige, the privilege, and the burden of command.

Captain MacWhirr could expect no relief of that sort from anyone on earth. Such is the loneliness of command. He was trying to see, with that watchful manner of a seaman who stares into the wind's eye as if into the eye of an adversary, to penetrate the hidden intention and guess the aim and force of the thrust. The strong wind swept at him out of a vast obscurity; he felt under his feet the uneasiness of his ship, and he could not even discern the shadow of her shape. He wished it were not so; and very still he waited, feeling stricken by a blind man's helplessness.

To be silent was natural to him, dark or shine. Jukes, at his elbow, was yelling cheerily in the gusts, "We must have got the worst of it at once, sir." A faint burst of lightning quivered all round, as if flashed into a cavern—into a black and secret chamber of the sea, with a floor of foaming crests.

It unveiled for a sinister, fluttering moment a ragged mass of clouds hanging low, the lurch of the long outlines of the ship, the black figures of men caught on the bridge, heads forward, as if petrified in the act of butting. The darkness palpitated down upon all this, and then the real thing came at last.

It was something formidable and swift, like the sudden smashing of a vial of wrath. It seemed to explode all round the ship with an overpowering concussion and a rush of great waters, as if an immense dam had been blown up to windward. In an instant the men lost touch of each other. This is the disintegrating power of a great wind: it isolates one from one's kind. An earthquake, a landslide, an avalanche, overtake a man incidentally, as it were—without passion. A furious gale attacks him like a personal enemy, tries to grasp his limbs, fastens upon his mind, seeks to rout his very spirit out of him.

Jukes was driven away from his commander. He fancied himself whirled a great distance through the air. Everything disappeared—

even, for a moment, his power of thinking; but his hand had found one of the rail stanchions. He was inclined to disbelieve the reality of this experience. Though young, he had seen some bad weather, and had never doubted his ability to imagine the worst; but this was so much beyond his powers of fancy that it appeared incompatible with the existence of any ship whatever. He would have been incredulous about himself in the same way, perhaps, had he not been so harassed by the necessity of exerting a wrestling effort against a force trying to tear him away from his hold. Moreover, the conviction of not being utterly destroyed returned to him through the sensations of being half drowned, bestially shaken, and partly choked.

It seemed to him he remained there precariously alone with the stanchion for a long, long time. The rain poured on him, flowed, drove in sheets. He breathed in gasps; and sometimes the water he swallowed was fresh and sometimes it was salt. For the most part he kept his eyes shut tight, as if suspecting his sight might be destroyed in the immense flurry of the elements. When he ventured to blink, he derived some moral support from the green gleam of the starboard light shining feebly upon the rain and spray. He was actually looking at it when its ray fell upon the uprearing sea which put it out. He saw the head of the wave topple over, adding the mite of its crash to the tremendous uproar raging around him, and almost at the same instant the stanchion was wrenched away from his embracing arms. After a crushing thump on his back he found himself suddenly afloat and borne upwards. His first irresistible notion was that the whole China Sea had climbed on the bridge. Then, more sanely, he concluded himself gone overboard. All the time he was being tossed, flung, and rolled in great volumes of water, he kept on repeating mentally the words: "My God! My God! My God! My God!"

All at once, in a revolt of misery and despair, he formed the crazy resolution to get out of that. And he began to thresh about with his arms and legs. But as soon as he commenced his struggles he discovered that he had become somehow mixed up with a face, an oilskin coat, somebody's boots. He clawed ferociously all these things in turn, lost them, found them again, lost them once more, and finally was himself caught in the clasp of a pair of stout arms. He returned the embrace round a thick solid body. He had found his captain.

They tumbled over and over, tightening their hug. Suddenly the water let them down with a brutal bang; and, stranded against the side of the wheelhouse, out of breath and bruised, they were left to stagger up in the wind and hold on where they could.

Jukes came out of it rather horrified, as though he had escaped some unparalleled outrage. It weakened his faith in himself. He started shouting aimlessly to the man he could feel near him in that fiendish blackness, "Is it you, sir? Is it?" And he heard in answer a voice, as if crying far away, from a very great distance, the one word "Yes!" Other seas swept again over the bridge. He received them defenselessly over his bare head, with both his hands engaged in holding.

The motion of the ship was extravagant. Her lurches had an appalling helplessness: she pitched as if taking a header into a void, and seemed to find a wall to hit every time. When she rolled she fell on her side headlong, and she would be righted back by such a demolishing blow that Jukes felt her reeling as a clubbed man reels before he collapses. And then she would begin her tumbling again as if dropped back into a boiling caldron.

The sea, flattened down in the heavier gusts, would uprise and overwhelm both ends of the *Nan-Shan* in snowy rushes of foam, expanding wide, beyond both rails, into the night. And on this dazzling sheet, spread under the blackness of the clouds and emitting a bluish glow, Captain MacWhirr could catch a desolate glimpse of a few tiny specks black as ebony, the tops of the hatches, the heads of winches, the foot of a mast. This was all he could see of his ship. Her middle structure, covered by the bridge which bore him, his mate, and the closed wheelhouse—her middle structure was like a half-tide rock awash upon a coast. It was like an outlying rock with the water boiling up, streaming over, pouring off—like a rock in the surf to which shipwrecked people cling before they let go—only it rose, it sank, it rolled continuously, like

a rock miraculously struck adrift from a coast and gone wallowing
upon the sea.

The *Nan-Shan* was being looted by the storm with a senseless,
destructive fury: awnings blown away, bridge swept clean, weather
cloths burst, rails twisted—and two of the boats had gone already.
They had gone unheard and unseen, melting, as it were, in the
shock and smother of the wave. It was only later, upon the white
flash of another high sea hurling itself amidships, that Jukes had
a vision of two pairs of davits leaping black and empty out of
the blackness. He poked his head forward, groping for the ear of
his commander. His lips touched it—big, fleshy, very wet. He
cried in an agitated tone, "Our boats are going, sir."

And again he heard that voice, forced and ringing feebly, but
with a penetrating effect of quietness in the enormous discord of
noises, as if sent out from some remote spot of peace beyond the
black wastes of the gale; again he heard it, and it was crying to
him, as if from very, very far— "All right."

He thought he had not managed to make himself understood.
"Our boats—I say boats, sir! Two gone!"

The same voice, within a foot of him and yet so remote, yelled
sensibly, "Can't be helped." Then Jukes caught some more words
in the wind. "What can—expect— Bound to leave—something
behind—stands to reason."

Watchfully Jukes listened for more. No more came. This was
all Captain MacWhirr had to say. An impenetrable obscurity
pressed down upon the ghostly glimmers of the sea. A dull conviction seized upon Jukes that there was nothing to be done.

If the steering gear did not give way, if the immense volumes
of water did not burst the deck in, if the engines did not give up,
if the ship did not bury herself in one of these awful seas whose
white crests he could see topping high above her bows—then
there was a chance of her coming out of it. Something within him
seemed to turn over, bringing uppermost the feeling that the *Nan-
Shan* was lost. "She's done for," he said to himself. One of these
things was bound to happen. Nothing could be prevented now;
the ship could not last. This weather was too impossible.

Jukes felt an arm thrown heavily over his shoulders; and to this overture he responded with great intelligence by catching hold of his captain round the waist.

They stood clasped thus in the blind night, bracing each other against the wind, cheek to cheek and lip to ear, in the manner of two hulks lashed stem to stern together.

And Jukes heard the voice of his commander, hardly any louder than before, but nearer, bearing that strange effect of quietness like the serene glow of a halo.

"D'ye know where the hands got to?" it asked, vigorous and evanescent at the same time.

Jukes didn't know. They had all been on the bridge when the real force of the hurricane had struck. He had no idea where they had crawled to. Under the circumstances they were nowhere, for all the use that could be made of them. Somehow the captain's wish to know distressed Jukes.

"Want the hands, sir?" he cried, apprehensively.

"Ought to know," asserted Captain MacWhirr. "Hold hard."

They held hard. An outburst of unchained fury, a vicious rush of the wind absolutely steadied the ship; she rocked only, quick and light like a child's cradle, for a terrific moment of suspense, while the whole atmosphere, as it seemed, streamed furiously past her, roaring away from the tenebrous earth.

It suffocated them, and with eyes shut they tightened their grasp. What from the magnitude of the shock might have been a column of water running upright in the dark, butted against the ship, broke short, and fell on her bridge, crushingly, from on high, with a dead burying weight.

A flying fragment of that collapse, a mere splash, enveloped them in one swirl from their feet over their heads, filling violently their ears, mouths, and nostrils with salt water. It knocked out their legs, wrenched at their arms, seethed away swiftly under their chins; and opening their eyes, they saw the piled-up masses of foam dashing to and fro amongst what looked like the fragments of a ship. She had given way as if driven straight in. Their panting hearts yielded, too, before the tremendous blow; and all at once she sprang up again to her desperate plunging, as if trying to scramble out from under the ruins.

The seas in the dark seemed to rush from all sides to keep her back where she might perish. There was hate in the way she was handled, and ferocity in the blows that fell. She was like a living creature thrown to the rage of a mob: struck at, borne up, flung down, leaped upon. Captain MacWhirr and Jukes kept hold of each other, deafened by the noise, gagged by the wind; and the great physical tumult beating about their bodies brought, like an unbridled display of passion, a profound trouble to their souls. One of those wild and appalling shrieks that are heard at times passing mysteriously overhead in the steady roar of a hurricane, swooped, as if borne on wings, upon the ship, and Jukes tried to outscream it.

"Will she live through this?"

The cry was wrenched out of his breast. It was as unintentional as the birth of a thought in the head. He heard nothing of it himself, and he expected nothing from it. Nothing at all. For indeed, what answer could be made? But after a while he heard with amazement the frail and resisting voice in his ear, the dwarf sound, unconquered in the giant tumult.

"She may!"

It was a dull yell, more difficult to seize than a whisper. And presently the voice returned again, half submerged in the vast crashes.

"Let's hope so!" it cried—small, lonely, and unmoved, a stranger to the visions of hope or fear; and it flickered into disconnected words: "Ship . . . This . . . Never— Anyhow . . . for the best." Jukes gave it up.

Then, as if it had come suddenly upon the one thing fit to withstand the power of a storm, it seemed to gain force for the last broken shouts:

"Builders . . . good men. . . . And chance it . . . engines. . . . Rout . . . good man."

Captain MacWhirr removed his arm from Jukes' shoulders, and thereby ceased to exist for his mate, so dark it was. Jukes, after a tense stiffening of every muscle, let himself go limp all over. Incredibly he felt disposed towards somnolence, as though he had been buffeted into drowsiness. The wind would get hold of his head and try to shake it off his shoulders; his clothes, full of water, were as heavy as lead, cold and dripping like an armor of melting ice: he shivered—it lasted a long time; and with his hands closed hard on his hold, he let himself sink slowly into the depths of bodily misery. His mind became concentrated upon himself in an aimless way, and when something pushed lightly at the back of his knees he nearly, as the saying is, jumped out of his skin.

In the start forward he bumped the back of Captain MacWhirr, who didn't move; and then a hand gripped his thigh. A lull had come, a menacing lull of the wind, the holding of a stormy breath—and he felt himself pawed all over. It was the boatswain. Jukes recognized these hands, so thick and enormous that they seemed to belong to some new species of man.

The boatswain had arrived on the bridge, crawling on all fours against the wind, and had found the chief mate's legs with the top of his head. Immediately he crouched and began to explore Jukes' person upwards with prudent, apologetic touches, as became an inferior.

He was an ill-favored, undersized, gruff sailor of fifty, coarsely hairy, short-legged, long-armed, resembling an elderly ape. His strength was immense, and in his great lumpy paws, bulging like brown boxing gloves on the end of furry forearms, the heaviest objects were handled like playthings. Apart from the grizzled pelt on his chest, his menacing demeanor and his hoarse voice, he had none of the classical attributes of the boatswain. His good nature almost amounted to imbecility: the men did what they liked with him, and he was easygoing and talkative. For these reasons Jukes disliked him; but Captain MacWhirr, to Jukes' disgust, seemed to regard him as a first-rate petty officer.

He pulled himself up by Jukes' coat, taking that liberty with the greatest moderation. "What is it, boss'n, what is it?" yelled Jukes, impatiently.

The typhoon had got on Jukes' nerves. The husky bellowings of

84

the other, though unintelligible, seemed to suggest a state of lively satisfaction. There could be no mistake. The old fool was pleased with something.

The boatswain's other hand had found some other body, for in a changed tone he began to inquire, "Is it you, sir? Is it you, sir?" The wind strangled his howls.

"Yes!" cried Captain MacWhirr.

CHAPTER IV

ALL THAT THE BOATSWAIN, yelling, could make clear to Captain MacWhirr was the bizarre intelligence that "All them Chinamen in the fore tween-deck have fetched away, sir."

Jukes, six inches to leeward, could hear these two shouting as you may hear on a still night half a mile away two men conversing across a field. He heard Captain MacWhirr's exasperated "What? What?" and the strained pitch of the other's hoarseness.

"In a lump . . . seen them myself. . . . Awful sight, sir . . . thought . . . tell you."

Jukes remained indifferent, as if rendered irresponsible by the force of the hurricane. The very thought of action seemed utterly vain. Besides, the occupation of keeping his heart completely steeled against the worst had become an engrossing one—so engrossing that he had come to feel an overpowering dislike towards any other form of activity whatever. He was not scared; he knew this because, firmly believing he would never see another sunrise, he remained calm in that belief. Even good men surrender at times to such moments of do-nothing heroics. And Jukes was a very young man. He conceived himself to be calm—inexorably calm—but as a matter of fact he was daunted; not abjectly, but only so far as a decent man may be daunted, without becoming loathsome to himself.

It was rather like a forced-on numbness of spirit. The long, long stress of a gale does it; and there is a bodily fatigue in the mere holding on to existence within the excessive tumult. Jukes was benumbed much more than he supposed. He held on—very wet, very cold; and in a momentary hallucination of swift visions (it is said that a drowning man thus reviews his life) he beheld all sorts of memories altogether unconnected with his present situation. He remembered his father, for instance: a worthy businessman who at an unfortunate crisis in his affairs went quietly to bed and died forthwith in a state of resignation. He also remembered a certain game of nap played when quite a boy on board a ship, since lost with all hands; he remembered the thick eyebrows of his first skipper; and without any emotion, as he might years ago have walked into her room and found her there with a book, he remembered his mother—dead, too, now—the resolute woman, left badly off, who had been very firm in his bringing up.

It could not have lasted more than a second. A heavy arm fell about his shoulders; Captain MacWhirr's voice was speaking.

"Jukes! Jukes!"

He detected the tone of deep concern. The wind had thrown its weight on the ship, trying to pin her down amongst the seas. The breakers flung out of the night, ferocious, boiling up, with a ghostly light of sea foam on their crests. The ship could not shake herself clear of the water; Jukes, rigid, perceived in her motion the ominous sign of haphazard floundering. She was no longer struggling intelligently. It was the beginning of the end; and the note of busy concern in Captain MacWhirr's voice sickened him like an exhibition of pernicious folly. Still Captain MacWhirr persisted in his cries. He hung round Jukes' neck as heavy as a millstone, and the sides of their heads knocked together.

"Jukes! Mr. Jukes, I say!"

He had to answer that voice that would not be silenced; and he did so in the customary manner: ". . . Yes, sir."

And directly, his heart, corrupted by the storm that breeds a craving for peace, rebelled. But Captain MacWhirr had his mate's head fixed firm in the crook of his elbow, and pressed it to his yelling lips.

". . . Says . . . whole lot . . . fetched away. . . . Ought to see . . . what's the matter."

Directly the full force of the hurricane had struck the ship, every part of her deck had become untenable; and the sailors, dazed and dismayed, had taken shelter in the port alleyway under the bridge. It was very black, cold, and dismal in the alleyway. At each fling of the ship they would groan all together in the dark, and tons of water could be heard scuttling about as if trying to get at them from above. The boatswain had been keeping up a gruff talk, but a more unreasonable lot of men, he said afterwards, he had never been with. They were snug enough there, out of harm's way; and yet they did nothing but complain peevishly like so many sick kids. Finally, one of them said that if there had been at least some light to see each other's noses by, it wouldn't be so bad. It was making him crazy, he declared, to lie there in the dark waiting for the blamed hooker to sink.

"Why don't you step outside, then, and be done with it at once?" the boatswain turned on him.

This called up a shout of execration. The boatswain found himself overwhelmed with reproaches. They seemed to take it ill that a lamp was not instantly created for them. They would whine after a light to get drowned by—anyhow! And though the unreason of their revilings was patent—since no one could hope to reach the lamp room, which was forward—he became greatly distressed. He did not think it was decent of them to nag at him like this. He sought refuge in an embittered silence, but at the same time their grumbling and muttering worried him greatly.

By and by it occurred to him that there were six globe lamps hung in the tween-deck, and that there could be no harm in depriving the coolies of one of them.

Now the *Nan-Shan* had an athwartship coal bunker which communicated by an iron door with the fore tween-deck. The bunker was empty of coal at this time, and its manhole was in the alleyway where the sailors had taken refuge. The boatswain could get to the tween-deck, therefore, without going out on deck at all. But to his great surprise he found he could induce no one to help him in taking off the manhole cover. He groped for it, but one of the crew lying in his way refused to budge.

"Why, I only want to get you that blamed light you're crying for," he expostulated, almost pitifully.

Somebody told him to go and put his head in a bag. He regretted he could not recognize the voice; otherwise, as he said, he would have put a head on *that* son of a sea cook. Nevertheless, he had made up his mind to show them he could get a light, if he were to die for it.

Through the violence of the ship's rolling, every movement was dangerous. He nearly broke his neck dropping into the bunker. He fell on his back, and was sent shooting helplessly from side to side in the dangerous company of a heavy iron bar—a coal trimmer's slice probably—left down there by somebody. This thing made him as nervous as though it had been a wild beast. He could not see it, the inside of the bunker being perfectly black; but he heard it sliding and clattering, and striking here and there, always in the neighborhood of his head. Meanwhile he was being flung from port to starboard and back again, and clawing desperately the smooth sides of the bunker in the endeavor to stop himself. The door into the tween-deck not fitting quite true, he saw a thread of dim light at the bottom.

Being a sailor, and a still active man, he did not want much of a chance to regain his feet; and as luck would have it, in scrambling up he put his hand on the iron slice. He picked it up as he rose. Otherwise he would have been afraid of the thing breaking his legs, or at least knocking him down again.

At first he stood still. He had struck his head twice; he was dazed a little; and he felt unsafe in this darkness that seemed to make the ship's motion unfamiliar, difficult to counteract. He was vaguely amazed at the plainness with which down there he could hear the gale raging. Its howls and shrieks seemed to take on, in the emptiness of the bunker, something of human rage and pain—being not vast but infinitely poignant. And there were, with every roll, thumps, too—profound, ponderous thumps, as if a bulky object of five-ton weight or so had got loose in the hold. But there was no such thing in the cargo. Something on deck? Impossible. Or alongside? Couldn't be.

He thought all this quickly, competently, like a seaman, and in the end remained puzzled. This other noise, though: was it the wind? Must be. It made down there a row like the shouting of a lot of crazed men. And he discovered in himself a desire for a light, too—if only to get drowned by—and a nervous anxiety to get out of that bunker as quickly as possible.

He pulled back the bolt. The heavy iron plate turned on its hinges; and it was as though he had opened the door to the sounds of the tempest. A gust of hoarse yelling met him; and the rushing of water overhead was covered by a tumult of strangled, throaty shrieks. He straddled his legs the whole width of the doorway and stretched his neck. At first he perceived only what he had come to seek: six small yellow flames swinging violently on the great body of the dusk.

The space he was looking at was stayed like the gallery of a mine, with a row of stanchions in the middle, and crossbeams overhead, penetrating into the gloom ahead—indefinitely. And to port there loomed, as if a side of the mine had caved in, a bulky mass with a slanting outline. The whole place, with the shadows and the shapes, moved all the time. The boatswain glared; then the ship lurched to starboard, and a great howl came from that mass that had the slant of fallen earth.

Pieces of wood whizzed past. Startled, the boatswain flung back his head. At his feet a man went sliding over, open-eyed, on his back, with uplifted arms; and another came bounding like a detached stone with his head between his legs and his hands clenched. His pigtail whipped in the air; he made a grab at the boatswain's legs, and from his opened hand a bright white disk rolled against the boatswain's foot. He recognized a silver dollar, and yelled at it with astonishment. With a sound of trampling and shuffling of bare feet, and with guttural cries, the mound of writhing bodies which had been piled up to port detached itself from the ship's side. Sliding, inert and struggling, it shifted to starboard, with a dull, brutal thump. The cries ceased. The boatswain heard a long moan through the roar and whistling of the wind; he saw an inextricable confusion of heads and shoulders, naked soles kicking upwards, fists raised, tumbling backs, legs, pigtails, faces.

"Good Lord!" he cried, horrified, and banged-to the iron door upon this vision.

This was what he had come on the bridge to tell. He could not keep it to himself; and on board ship there is only one man to whom it is worthwhile to unburden yourself. On his passage back the hands in the alleyway swore at him. Why didn't he bring that lamp? What the devil did the coolies matter? And when he came out, the extremity of the ship made what went on inside of her appear of little moment.

At first he thought he had left the alleyway in the very moment of her sinking. The bridge ladders had been washed away, but an enormous sea, filling the afterdeck, floated him up to the bridge. After that he had to lie on his stomach for some time, holding to a ringbolt, swallowing salt water. He struggled farther on his hands and knees, too frightened to turn back. In this way he reached the afterpart of the wheelhouse. In that comparatively sheltered spot he found the second mate. The boatswain was pleasantly surprised—his impression being that everybody on deck must have been washed away long ago. He asked eagerly where the Captain was.

The second mate was lying low, like a malignant little animal under a hedge.

"Captain? Gone overboard, after getting us into this mess." The mate, too, for all he knew or cared. Another fool.

The boatswain crawled out again into the wind; not because he much expected to find anybody, he said, but just to get away from "that man." He crawled out as outcasts go to face an inclement world. Hence his great joy at finding Jukes and the Captain. But what was going on in the tween-deck was to him a minor matter by that time. Besides, it was difficult to make yourself heard. But he managed to convey the idea that the Chinamen had broken adrift together with their boxes, and that he had come up on purpose to report this. As to the hands, they were all right. Then, appeased, he subsided on the deck in a sitting posture, hugging with his arms and legs the stand of the engine-room telegraph—an iron casting as thick as a post. When that went, why, he expected he would go, too. He gave no more thought to the coolies.

CAPTAIN MACWHIRR HAD MADE Jukes understand that he wanted him to go down below—to see.

"What am I to do then, sir?" And the trembling of his whole wet body caused Jukes' voice to sound like bleating.

"See first . . . Boss'n . . . says . . . adrift."

"That boss'n is a confounded fool," howled Jukes, shakily.

The absurdity of the demand made upon him revolted Jukes. He was as unwilling to go as if the moment he had left the deck the ship were sure to sink.

"I must know . . . can't leave. . . ." yelled MacWhirr.

"They'll settle, sir."

"Fight . . . boss'n says they fight. . . . Why? Can't have . . . fighting . . . board ship. . . . Much rather keep you here . . . case . . . I should . . . washed overboard myself. . . . Stop it . . . some way. You see and tell me . . . through engine-room tube. Don't want you . . . come up here . . . too often. Dangerous . . . moving about."

Jukes, held with his head in chancery, had to listen.

". . . Rout. . . . Good man. . . . Ship . . . may . . . through this . . . all right yet."

All at once Jukes understood he would have to go.

"Do you think she may?" he screamed.

But the wind devoured the reply, out of which Jukes heard only the one word, pronounced with great energy ". . . Always. . . ."

Captain MacWhirr released Jukes, and bending over the boatswain, yelled, "Get back with the mate." Jukes only knew that the arm was gone off his shoulders. He was dismissed with his orders—to do what? He was exasperated into letting go his hold carelessly, and on the instant was blown away. He flung himself down hastily, and the boatswain, who was following, fell on him.

"Don't *you* get up yet, sir," cried the boatswain. "No hurry!"

A sea swept over. Jukes understood the boatswain to splutter that the bridge ladders were gone. "I'll lower you down, sir, by your hands," he screamed. He shouted also something about the smokestack being as likely to go overboard as not. Jukes imagined the fires out, the ship helpless. . . . The boatswain by his side kept on yelling. "What? What is it?" Jukes cried distressfully; and the other repeated, "What would my old woman say if she saw me now?"

In the alleyway, where a lot of water had got in and splashed in the dark, the men were still as death, till Jukes stumbled against one of them and cursed him savagely for being in the way. Two or three voices then asked, eager and weak, "Any chance for us, sir?"

"What's the matter with you fools?" he said brutally. But they seemed cheered; and in the midst of obsequious warnings, "Look out! Mind that manhole lid, sir," they lowered him into the bunker. The boatswain tumbled down after him, and as soon as the boatswain had picked himself up Jukes remarked, "She would say, 'Serve you right, you old fool, for going to sea.'"

The boatswain had some means, and made a point of alluding to them frequently. His wife—a fat woman—and two grown-up daughters kept a greengrocer's shop in the East End of London.

In the dark, Jukes, unsteady on his legs, listened to a faint thunderous patter. A deadened screaming went on steadily at his elbow, as it were. His head swam. To him, too, in that bunker, the motion of the ship seemed novel and menacing, sapping his resolution.

He had half a mind to scramble out again; but the remembrance of Captain MacWhirr's voice made this impossible. His orders were to go and see. Enraged, he told himself he would see—of course. But the boatswain, staggering, warned him to be careful how he opened that door; there was a blamed fight going on. Jukes desired irritably to know what the devil they were fighting for.

"Dollars! Dollars, sir. All their rotten chests got burst open. Blamed money skipping all over the place, and they are tumbling after it head over heels—tearing and biting like anything. A regular little hell in there."

Jukes convulsively opened the door. The short boatswain peered under his arm.

One of the lamps had gone out, broken perhaps. Rancorous, guttural cries burst on their ears, and a strange panting sound. A hard blow hit the side of the ship; water fell above with a stunning shock, and in the forefront of the gloom, where the air was reddish and thick, Jukes saw a head bang the deck violently, two thick calves waving on high, muscular arms twined round a naked body, a yellow face, openmouthed and with a set wild stare, look up and slide away. An empty chest clattered turning over; a man fell head first with a jump, as if lifted by a kick; and farther off, indistinct, others streamed like a mass of rolling stones down a bank, thumping the deck with their feet and flourishing their arms wildly. The hatchway ladder was loaded with coolies swarming on it like bees on a branch. They hung on the steps in a crawling, stirring cluster, beating madly with their fists the underside of the battened hatch, and the headlong rush of the water above was heard in the intervals of their yelling. The ship heeled over more, and they began to drop off: first one, then two, then all the rest went away together, falling straight off with a great cry.

Jukes was confounded. The boatswain, with gruff anxiety, begged him, "Don't you go in there, sir."

The whole place seemed to twist upon itself. The ship rose to a sea, and Jukes fancied that all these men would be shot upon him in a body. He backed out, swung the door to, and with trembling hands pushed at the bolt. . . .

As soon as his mate had gone Captain MacWhirr, left alone on the bridge, sidled and staggered as far as the wheelhouse. He had to fight the gale to open the door, and when at last he managed to enter, it was with a clatter and a bang, as though he had been fired through the wood. He stood within, holding on to the handle.

The steering gear leaked steam, and in the confined space the glass of the binnacle made a shiny oval of light in a thin white fog. The wind howled with sudden booming gusts that rattled the doors and shutters. With every sweeping blow of a sea, water squirted violently through the cracks all round the door. The man at the helm had flung down his cap, his coat, and stood propped against the gear casing in a striped cotton shirt open on his breast. The little brass wheel in his hands had the appearance of a bright and fragile toy. The cords of his neck stood hard and lean, and his face was still and sunken as in death.

Captain MacWhirr wiped his eyes. The sea that had nearly taken him overboard had, to his annoyance, washed off his sou'wester hat. The fluffy, fair hair, soaked and darkened, resembled a mean skein of cotton threads festooned round his bare skull. His face, glistening with seawater, had been made crimson with the wind.

"You here?" he muttered, heavily.

The second mate had found his way into the wheelhouse. He had fixed himself in a corner with his knees up, a fist pressed against each temple; and this attitude suggested rage, resignation, and a sort of concentrated unforgiveness. He said defiantly, "Well, it's my watch below now, ain't it?"

The steam gear clattered, stopped, clattered again; and the helmsman's eyeballs seemed to project out of his face towards the compass card behind the binnacle glass. God knows how long he had been left there to steer, as if forgotten by all his shipmates. The bells had not been struck; the ship's routine had gone down-wind; but he was trying to keep her head north-northeast. The rudder might have been gone for all he knew, the fires out, the ship ready to roll over like a corpse. He was anxious not to get muddled and lose control of her head, because the compass card swung both ways, wriggling, and sometimes seemed to whirl right round. He suffered from mental stress. He was horribly afraid, also, of the wheelhouse going. Mountains of water kept on tumbling against it. When the ship took one of her desperate dives the corners of his lips twitched.

Captain MacWhirr looked up at the wheelhouse clock. It was half past one in the morning.

"Another day," he muttered to himself.

The second mate heard him. "You won't see it break," he

exclaimed. His wrists and his knees shook violently. "No, by God! You won't. . . ."

The body of the helmsman moved slightly, but his head didn't budge on his neck—like a stone head fixed to look one way from a column. Captain MacWhirr said austerely, "Don't you pay any attention to what that man says." And then, with an indefinable change of tone, very grave, he added, "He isn't on duty."

The sailor said nothing. The hurricane boomed, shaking the little place; and the light of the binnacle flickered.

"You haven't been relieved," Captain MacWhirr went on, looking down. "I want you to stick to the helm, though, as long as you can. You've got the hang of her. And the hands are probably busy with a job down below. . . . Think you can?"

The steering gear leaped into an abrupt short clatter. The still man burst out, as if all the passion in him had gone into his lips: "By heavens, sir! I can steer forever if nobody talks to me."

"Oh! Aye! All right . . ." The Captain lifted his eyes for the first time to the man, ". . . Hackett."

And he seemed to dismiss this matter from his mind. He stooped to the engine-room speaking tube, blew in, and bent his head. Mr. Rout below answered, and at once Captain MacWhirr put his lips to the mouthpiece.

With the uproar of the gale around him he applied alternately his lips and his ear, and the engineer's voice mounted to him harshly. One of the stokers was disabled, the others had given in, the second engineer and the donkeyman were firing up. The third engineer was standing by the steam valve. The engines were being tended by hand. How was it above?

"Bad enough. It mostly rests with you," said Captain MacWhirr. Was the mate down there yet? No? Well, he would be presently. Would Mr. Rout let him talk through the speaking tube—through the deck speaking tube, because he—the Captain—was going out again on the bridge. There was some trouble amongst the Chinamen. They were fighting, it seemed. Couldn't allow fighting. . . .

Mr. Rout had gone away, and Captain MacWhirr could feel

against his ear the pulsation of the engines, like the beat of the ship's heart. Mr. Rout's voice down there shouted something distantly. The ship pitched headlong, and the pulsation stopped dead. Captain MacWhirr's face was impassive, and his eyes were fixed aimlessly on the crouching shape of the second mate. Again Mr. Rout's voice cried out in the depths, and the pulsating beats recommenced.

Mr. Rout had returned to the tube. "She takes these dives as if she never meant to come up again," he said, with irritation. "Don't let me drive her under."

"Dark and rain. Can't see what's coming," said the Captain's voice from above. "Must—keep—her—moving—enough to steer—and chance it," it went on. "We are—getting—smashed up—a good deal up here. Doing—fairly well, though. Of course—if the wheelhouse should go . . ."

Mr. Rout, bending an attentive ear, muttered peevishly. Then the deliberate voice up there asked, "Jukes turned up yet?" After a short wait it continued, "I wish he would bear a hand. I want him up here in case of anything. I am all alone. The second mate's lost. . . ."

"What?" shouted Mr. Rout, taking his head away. "Gone overboard?" and clapped his ear to the tube.

"Lost his nerve," the voice from above continued in a matter-of-fact tone. "Damned awkward."

Mr. Rout, listening, opened his eyes wide at this. However, he heard something like the sounds of a scuffle and broken exclamations coming down to him. He strained his hearing; and all the time, Beale, the third engineer, with his arms uplifted, held between the palms of his hands the rim of a little black wheel projecting at the side of a big copper pipe. He seemed to be poising it above his head, as though it was a correct attitude in some sort of game.

His smooth cheek was begrimed and flushed, and the coal dust on his eyelids, like the black penciling of a makeup, enhanced the liquid brilliance of the whites, giving to his youthful face something of a feminine, exotic aspect. When the ship pitched he would with hasty movements of his hands screw hard at the little wheel.

"Gone crazy," began the Captain's voice suddenly in the tube.

"Rushed at me. . . . Just now. Had to knock him down. . . . This minute. You heard, Mr. Rout?"

"The devil!" muttered Mr. Rout. "Look out, Beale!"

His shout rang out like the blast of a warning trumpet, between the iron walls of the engine room. Painted white, they rose high into the dusk of the skylight, sloping like a roof; and the whole lofty space resembled the interior of a monument, divided by floors of iron grating, with lights flickering at different levels. The whole loftiness of the place, booming hollow to the great voice of the wind, was swaying at the top like a tree about to go over bodily. Beale frantically turned his little wheel. At the same moment Jukes appeared in the stokehold doorway.

"You've got to hurry up," shouted Mr. Rout, as soon as he saw Jukes.

Jukes' glance was wandering and tipsy; his red face was puffy, as though he had overslept. He had had an arduous road, and had traveled over it with immense vivacity. He had rushed up out of the bunker, stumbling in the dark alleyway amongst a lot of bewildered men who, trod upon, asked "What's up, sir?" in awed mutters; and then he had clambered down the stokehold ladder, missing many iron rungs in his hurry, down into a place deep as a well, black as Tophet, tipping back and forth like a seesaw. The water in the bilges thundered at each roll, and lumps of coal skipped to and fro, from end to end, rattling like an avalanche of pebbles. Under each of six fire doors was a glow like a pool of flaming blood radiating in blackness. The stokehold ventilators hummed; and in front of the six fire doors two wild figures, stripped to the waist, staggered and stooped, wrestling with two shovels.

"Hallo! Plenty of draft now," yelled the second engineer, as though he had been all the time looking out for Jukes. The donkeyman, a dapper little chap with fair skin and a tiny mustache, worked in a sort of mute transport. They were keeping up a full head of steam. "Blowing off all the time," went on yelling the second; and with a sound as of a hundred scoured saucepans, the orifice of a ventilator spat upon his shoulder a sudden gush of salt water. He volleyed out a stream of curses. "Where's the blooming ship? Can you tell me? Blast my eyes! Underwater—or what? Hey? Don't you know anything—you jolly sailorman you . . . ?"

Jukes, after a bewildered moment, had been helped by a roll to dart through the stokehold, past the second engineer, but as soon as his eyes took in the comparative vastness and peace of the engine room, the ship, setting her stern heavily in the water, sent him charging head down upon Mr. Rout. The chief's arm, long like a tentacle, went out to meet him. At the same time Mr. Rout repeated:

"You've got to hurry up, whatever it is."

Jukes yelled into a speaking tube, "Are you there, sir?" and listened. Nothing. The roar of the wind fell straight into his ear, but presently a small voice shoved the hurricane aside.

"You, Jukes? Well?"

Jukes was ready to talk; it was only time that seemed to be wanting. It was easy enough to account for everything. He could perfectly imagine the coolies battened down in the tween-deck, lying sick and scared between the rows of chests. Then he could imagine one of these chests—or perhaps several at once—breaking loose in a roll, knocking out others, lids flying open, and all the Chinamen rising up to save their property. Afterwards every fling of the ship would hurl that yelling mob here and there, from side to side, in a whirl of smashed wood, torn clothing, rolling dollars. A struggle once started, they would be unable to stop themselves. Nothing could stop them now except main force. It was a disaster. He had seen it, and that was all he could say. Some of them must be dead, he believed. The rest would go on fighting. . . .

Jukes wanted only to be dismissed from the face of that odious trouble intruding on the great need of the ship. He sent up his words, tripping over each other, crowding the narrow tube. They mounted as if into a silence of an enlightened comprehension dwelling alone up there with a storm.

CHAPTER V

HE WAITED. BEFORE HIS EYES the engines turned with slow labor, that in the moment of going off into a mad fling would stop dead at Mr. Rout's shout, "Look out, Beale!" They would pause then in an intelligent immobility, stilled in midstroke, a heavy crank arrested on the cant, as if conscious of danger. Then, with a "Now, then!" from the chief, and the sound of a breath expelled through clenched teeth, they would accomplish the interrupted revolution and begin another.

There was the prudent sagacity of wisdom and the deliberation of enormous strength in their movements. This was their work— this patient coaxing of a distracted ship over the fury of the waves. At times Mr. Rout's chin would sink on his breast, and he watched them with knitted eyebrows as if lost in thought. He was fighting this fight in a pair of carpet slippers. A short shiny jacket barely covered his loins, and his white wrists protruded far out of the tight sleeves, as though the emergency had added to his stature, lengthened his limbs, augmented his pallor, hollowed his eyes.

The voice that kept the hurricane out of Jukes' ear began: "Take the hands with you . . ." and left off unexpectedly.

"What could I do with them, sir?"

A harsh, abrupt, imperious clang exploded suddenly. The three pairs of eyes flew up to the dial of the engine-room telegraph. The hand on the dial jumped from FULL SPEED AHEAD to STOP, as if snatched by a devil. And then these three men in the engine room had the intimate sensation of a check upon the ship, of a strange shrinking, as if she had gathered herself for a desperate leap.

"Stop her!" bellowed Mr. Rout.

Nobody—not even Captain MacWhirr, who alone on deck had caught sight of a white line of foam coming on at such a height that he couldn't believe his eyes—nobody was to know the steepness of that sea and the awful depth of the hollow the hurricane had scooped out behind the running wall of water.

It raced to meet the ship, and, with a pause, as of girding the loins, the *Nan-Shan* lifted her bows and leaped. The flames in all the lamps sank, darkening the engine room. One went out. With a tearing crash and a swirling, raving tumult, tons of water fell upon the deck, as though the ship had darted under the foot of a cataract.

Down there they looked at each other, stunned.

"Swept from end to end, by God!" bawled Jukes.

She dipped into the hollow straight down, as if going over the edge of the world. The engine room toppled forward menacingly, like the inside of a tower nodding in an earthquake. An awful racket, of iron things falling, came from the stokehold. She hung on this appalling slant long enough for Beale to drop on his hands and knees and begin to crawl as if he meant to fly on all fours out of the engine room, and for Mr. Rout to turn his head slowly, rigid, cavernous, with the lower jaw dropping. Jukes had shut his eyes, and his face in a moment became hopelessly blank and gentle, like the face of a blind man.

At last she rose slowly, staggering, as if she had to lift a mountain with her bows.

Mr. Rout shut his mouth; Jules blinked; and little Beale stood up hastily.

"Another one like this, and that's the last of her," cried the chief.

He and Jukes looked at each other, and the same thought came into their heads. The Captain! Everything must have been swept away. Steering gear gone—ship like a log. All over directly.

"Rush!" ejaculated Mr. Rout thickly, glaring with enlarged, doubtful eyes at Jukes, who answered him by an irresolute glance.

The clang of the telegraph gong soothed them instantly. The black hand dropped from STOP to FULL.

"Now then, Beale!" cried Mr. Rout.

The steam hissed low. The piston rods slid in and out. Jukes put his ear to the tube. The voice was ready for him. It said, "Pick up all the money. Bear a hand now. I'll want you up here." And that was all.

"Sir?" called up Jukes. There was no answer.

He staggered away like a defeated man from the field of battle.

He had got, in some way or other, a cut above his left eyebrow—a cut to the bone. He was not aware of it in the least; quantities of the China Sea, large enough to break his neck for him, had gone over his head, had cleaned, washed, and salted the wound. It did not bleed, but only gaped red; and this gash over the eye, his disheveled hair, the disorder of his clothes, gave him the aspect of a man worsted in a fight with fists.

"Got to pick up the dollars." He appealed to Mr. Rout, smiling pitifully at random.

"What's that?" asked Mr. Rout, wildly. "Pick up . . . ? I don't care. . . ." Then, quivering in every muscle, but with an exaggeration of paternal tone, "Go away now, for God's sake. You deck people'll drive me silly. There's that second mate been going for the old man. Don't you know? You fellows are going wrong for want of something to do. . . ."

At these words Jukes discovered in himself the beginnings of anger. Want of something to do, indeed. . . . Full of hot scorn against the chief, he turned to go the way he had come. In the stokehold the donkeyman toiled with his shovel mutely, but the second was carrying on like a noisy, undaunted maniac.

"Hallo, you wandering officer! Hey! Can't you get some of your slush-slingers to wind up a few of them ashes? I am getting choked with them here. Curse it! Hey! Remember the articles: *Sailors and firemen to assist each other*. Hey! D'ye hear?"

Jukes climbed out frantically. A frenzy possessed him. By the time he was back amongst the men in the darkness of the alleyway, he felt ready to wring all their necks at the slightest sign of hanging back. The very thought of it exasperated him. *He* couldn't hang back. They shouldn't.

The impetuosity with which he came amongst them carried them along. They had already been excited and startled at all his comings and goings; he appeared formidable—busied with matters of life and death that brooked no delay. At his first word they dragged into the bunker one after another obediently, though they were not clear as to what was to be done. "What is it? What is it?" they asked each other.

The boatswain tried to explain; the sounds of a great scuffle surprised them; and the mighty shocks, reverberating in the black bunker, kept them in mind of their danger. When the boatswain threw open the door it seemed that an eddy of the hurricane, stealing through the iron sides of the ship, had set all these bodies whirling like dust; there came to them a confused uproar, a tempestuous tumult, gusts of screams, and the tramping of feet mingling with the blows of the sea.

For a moment they glared amazed, blocking the doorway. Jukes pushed through them brutally. He said nothing, and simply darted in. Another lot of coolies on the ladder, struggling suicidally to break through the battened hatch to a swamped deck, fell off as before, and he disappeared under them like a man overtaken by a landslide.

The boatswain yelled excitedly, "Come along. Get the mate out. He'll be trampled to death. Come on."

They charged in, stamping on breasts, on fingers, on faces, catching their feet in clothing, kicking broken wood; but before they could get hold of him Jukes emerged waist-deep in a multitude of clawing hands. In the instant he had been lost to view, all the buttons of his jacket had gone, its back had split up to the collar, his waistcoat had been torn open. The central struggling mass of Chinamen went over to the roll, dark, indistinct, helpless, with a wild gleam of many eyes in the dim light of the lamps.

"Leave me alone—damn you. I am all right," screeched Jukes. "Drive them forward. Watch your chance when she pitches. Drive them against the bulkhead. Jam 'em up."

The rush of the sailors into the seething tween-deck was like a splash of cold water into a boiling caldron. The commotion sank for a moment.

The bulk of Chinamen were locked in such a compact scrimmage that, linking their arms and aided by an appalling dive of the ship, the seamen sent it forward in one great shove, like a solid block. Behind their backs small clusters and loose bodies tumbled from side to side.

The boatswain performed prodigious feats of strength. With

his long arms open, and each great paw clutching at a stanchion, he stopped the rush of seven entwined Chinamen rolling like a boulder. His joints cracked; he said, "Ha!" and they flew apart. But the carpenter showed the greater intelligence. Without saying a word to anybody he went back into the alleyway, to fetch several coils of cargo gear he had seen there—chain and rope. With these, lifelines were rigged.

There was really no resistance. The struggle, however it began, had turned into a scramble of blind panic. If the coolies had started up after their scattered dollars they were by that time fighting only for their footing. They took each other by the throat merely to save themselves from being hurled about. Whoever got a hold anywhere would kick at the others who caught at his legs and hung on, till a roll sent them flying together across the deck.

The coming of the white devils was a terror. Had they come to kill? The individuals torn out of the ruck became very limp in the seamen's hands; some, dragged aside by the heels, were passive, like dead bodies, with open, fixed eyes. Here and there a coolie would fall on his knees as if begging for mercy; several, whom the excess of fear made unruly, were hit with hard fists between the eyes, and cowered; while those who were hurt submitted to rough handling, blinking rapidly without a plaint. Faces streamed with blood; there were raw places on the shaven heads, bruises, torn wounds, gashes. The broken porcelain out of the chests was mostly responsible for the latter. Here and there a Chinaman, wild-eyed, with his tail unplaited, nursed a bleeding sole.

They had been ranged closely, after having been shaken into submission, cuffed a little to allay excitement, addressed in gruff words of encouragement that sounded like promises of evil. They sat on the deck in ghastly, drooping rows, and at the end the carpenter, with two hands to help him, moved busily from place to place, setting taut and hitching the lifelines. The boatswain, with one leg and one arm embracing a stanchion, struggled with a lamp pressed to his breast, trying to get a light, and growling all the time like an industrious gorilla. The figures of seamen stooped repeatedly, with the movements of gleaners, and everything was being flung into the bunker: clothing, smashed wood, broken china, and the dollars, too, gathered up in men's jackets. Now and then a sailor would stagger towards the doorway with his arms full of rubbish; and dolorous, slanting eyes followed his movements.

With every roll of the ship the long rows of sitting Chinamen would sway forward brokenly, and her headlong dives knocked together the line of shaven polls from end to end. When the wash of water rolling on the deck died away for a moment, it seemed to Jukes, yet quivering from his exertions, that in his mad struggle down there he had overcome the wind somehow: that a silence had fallen upon the ship, a silence in which the sea struck thunderously at her sides.

Everything had been cleared out of the tween-deck—all the wreckage, as the men said. They stood erect and tottering above the level of heads and drooping shoulders. Here and there a coolie sobbed for his breath. Where the high light fell, Jukes could see the salient ribs of one, the yellow, wistful face of another; bowed necks; or would meet a dull stare directed at his face. He was amazed that there had been no corpses; but the lot of them seemed at their last gasp, and they appeared to him more pitiful than if they had been all dead.

Suddenly one of the coolies began to speak. The light came and went on his lean, straining face; he threw his head up like a baying hound. From the bunker came the sounds of knocking and the tinkle of some dollars rolling loose; he stretched out his arm, his mouth yawned black, and the incomprehensible guttural hooting sounds that did not seem to belong to a human language penetrated Jukes with a strange emotion, as if a brute had tried to be eloquent.

Two more started mouthing what seemed to Jukes fierce denunciations; the others stirred with grunts and growls. Jukes ordered the hands out of the tween-decks hurriedly. He left last himself, backing through the door, while the grunts rose to a loud murmur and hands were extended after him as after a malefactor.

The boatswain shot the bolt, and remarked uneasily, "Seems as if the wind had dropped, sir."

The seamen were glad to get back into the alleyway. Secretly each of them thought that at the last moment he could rush out on deck—and that was a comfort. There is something horribly repugnant in the idea of being drowned under a deck. Now they had done with the Chinamen, they again became conscious of the ship's position.

Jukes on coming out of the alleyway found himself up to the neck in water. He gained the bridge, and discovered he could detect obscure shapes as if his sight had become preternaturally acute. He saw faint outlines. They recalled not the familiar aspect of the *Nan-Shan*, but something remembered—an old dismantled steamer he had seen years ago rotting on a mudbank. She recalled that wreck.

There was no wind, not a breath, except the faint currents created by the lurches of the ship. The smoke tossed out of the funnel was settling down upon the deck. He breathed it as he passed forward. He felt the deliberate throb of the engines, and heard small sounds that seemed to have survived the great uproar: the knocking of broken fittings, the tumbling of some piece of wreckage on the bridge. The unexpected stillness of the air oppressed Jukes.

He perceived dimly the squat shape of his captain holding on to a twisted bridge rail, motionless and swaying as if rooted to the planks.

"We have done it, sir," he gasped.

"Thought you would," said Captain MacWhirr.

"Did you?" murmured Jukes to himself.

"Wind fell all at once," went on the Captain.

Jukes burst out, "If you think it was an easy job—"

But his captain, clinging to the rail, paid no attention. "According to the books the worst is not over yet."

"If most of them hadn't been half dead with seasickness and fright, not one of us would have come out of that tween-deck alive," said Jukes.

"Had to do what's fair by them," mumbled MacWhirr, stolidly. "You don't find everything in books."

"Why, I believe they would have risen on us if I hadn't ordered the hands out," continued Jukes.

After the whisper of their shouts, their ordinary tones, so distinct, rang out very loud to their ears in the amazing stillness of the air. It seemed to them they were talking in a dark and echoing vault.

Through a jagged aperture in the dome of clouds the light of a few stars fell upon the black sea, rising and falling confusedly. The *Nan-Shan* wallowed heavily at the bottom of a circular cistern of clouds. This ring of dense vapors, gyrating madly round the calm of the center, encompassed the ship like a motionless wall, a wall whose aspect was inconceivably sinister. Within, the sea, as if agitated by an internal commotion, leaped in peaked mounds that jostled each other, slapping heavily against the ship's sides; and a low moaning sound, the infinite plaint of the storm's fury, came from beyond the limits of the menacing calm. Captain Mac-Whirr remained silent, and Jukes' ready ear caught suddenly the faint, long-drawn roar of some immense wave rushing unseen under that thick blackness.

"Of course," he started resentfully, "they thought we had caught at the chance to plunder them. Of course! You said—pick up the money. Easier said than done. They couldn't tell what was in our heads. We came in, smash—right into the middle of them. Had to do it by a rush."

"As long as it's done . . ." mumbled the Captain. "Had to do what's fair."

"We shall find yet there's the devil to pay when this is over," said Jukes, feeling very sore. "Let them only recover a bit, and you'll see. They will fly at our throats, sir. Don't forget, sir, she isn't a British ship now. These brutes know it, too. The damned Siamese flag."

"We are on board, all the same," remarked MacWhirr.

"The trouble's not over yet," insisted Jukes, prophetically, reeling and catching on. "She's a wreck," he added, faintly.

"The trouble's not over yet," assented Captain MacWhirr, half aloud. . . . "Look out for her a minute."

"Are you going off the deck, sir?" asked Jukes, hurriedly, as if the storm were sure to pounce upon him as soon as he had been left alone with the ship.

He watched her, battered and solitary, laboring heavily in a wild scene of mountainous black waters lit by the gleams of distant worlds. She moved slowly, breathing into the still core of the hurricane the excess of her strength in a white cloud of steam— and the deep-toned vibration of the escaping steam was like the defiant trumpeting of a living creature. It ceased suddenly. The still air moaned. Above Jukes' head a few stars shone into a pit of black vapors. The inky edge of the clouds frowned down upon the ship. The stars, too, seemed to look at her intently, as if for the last time, and the cluster of their splendor sat like a diadem on a lowering brow.

Captain MacWhirr had gone into the chart room. There was no light there; but he could feel the disorder of that place where he used to live tidily. His armchair was upset. The books had tumbled on the floor; he scrunched a piece of glass under his boot. He groped for matches and found a box on a shelf with a deep ledge. He struck one, and puckering his eyes, held out the little flame towards the barometer whose glittering top of glass and metals nodded at him.

It stood very low—incredibly low, so low that Captain Mac-Whirr grunted. The match went out, and hurriedly he extracted another. Again a little flame flared up before the nodding glass and metal. His eyes looked at it, narrowed with attention. With his grave face he resembled a booted and misshapen pagan burning incense before the oracle of a joss. There was no mistake. It was the lowest reading he had ever seen in his life.

Captain MacWhirr emitted a low whistle. He forgot himself till the flame diminished to a blue spark, burnt his fingers and vanished. Perhaps something had gone wrong with the thing!

There was a second barometer, an aneroid glass screw, above the couch. He turned that way, struck another match, and discovered the white face of the other instrument looking at him from the bulkhead, meaningly, not to be gainsaid. There was no room for doubt now. Captain MacWhirr pshawed and threw the match down.

The worst was to come, then—and if the books were right this worst would be very bad. The experience of the last six hours had enlarged his conception of what heavy weather could be like. "It'll be terrific," he pronounced, mentally.

He had not consciously looked at anything by the light of the matches except the barometer; and yet somehow he had seen that his water bottle and the two tumblers had been flung out of their stand. It seemed to give him a more intimate knowledge of the tossing the ship had gone through. "I wouldn't have believed it," he thought. And his table had been cleared, too; his rulers, his pencils, the inkstand—all the things that had their safe appointed places—they were gone, as if a mischievous hand had plucked them out one by one and flung them on the floor.

The hurricane had broken in upon the orderly arrangements of his privacy. This had never happened before, and the feeling of dismay reached the very seat of his composure. And the worst was to come yet! He was glad the trouble in the tween-deck had been discovered in time. If the ship had to go after all, then, at least, she wouldn't be going to the bottom with a lot of people in her fighting teeth and claw. That would have been odious.

These instantaneous thoughts were yet in their essence heavy and slow, partaking of the nature of the man. He extended his hand to put back the matchbox in its corner of the shelf. There were always matches there—by his order. The steward had his instructions impressed upon him long before. "A box . . . just there, see? . . . Not so very full . . . where I can put my hand on it, steward. Might want a light in a hurry. Can't tell on a ship *what* you might want in a hurry. Mind, now."

And of course on his side he would be careful to put it back in its place scrupulously. He did so now, but before he removed his hand it occurred to him that perhaps he would never have occasion to use that box anymore. The vividness of the thought checked him, and for a fraction of a second his fingers closed again on the small object, as though it had been the symbol of all the little habits that chain us to the round of life. He released it at last, and letting himself fall on the settee, listened for the first sounds of returning wind.

Not yet. He heard only the wash of water, the heavy splashes of confused seas.

But the quietude of the air was startlingly tense and unsafe, like a slender hair holding a sword suspended over his head. By this awful pause the storm penetrated the defenses of the man and unsealed his lips. He spoke out in the solitude and pitch-darkness of the cabin, as if addressing another being awakened within his breast.

"I shouldn't like to lose her," he said half aloud.

He sat unseen, apart from the sea, from his ship, isolated, as if withdrawn from the very current of his own existence. His palms reposed on his knees, and he bowed his short neck and puffed heavily, surrendering to a strange sensation of weariness.

From where he sat he could reach the door of a washstand locker. There should have been a towel there. There was. Good. . . . He took it out, wiped his face, and afterwards went on rubbing his wet head. He toweled himself with energy in the dark, and then remained motionless with the towel on his knees. A moment passed, of a stillness so profound that no one could have guessed there was a man sitting in that cabin. Then a murmur arose.

"She may come out of it yet."

When Captain MacWhirr came out on deck, which he did brusquely, as though he had suddenly become conscious of having stayed away too long, the calm had lasted already more than fifteen minutes—long enough to make itself intolerable even to his imagination. Jukes, motionless on the forepart of the bridge, began to speak at once. His voice sounded blank and forced as though he were talking through hard-set teeth.

"I had the wheel relieved. Hackett began to sing out that he was done. At first I couldn't get anybody to crawl out and relieve the poor devil. That boss'n's worse than no good. Thought I'd have had to go myself and haul out one of them by the neck."

"Ah, well," muttered the Captain, standing by Jukes' side.

"The second mate's in there, too, holding his head. Is he hurt, sir?"

"No—crazy," said Captain MacWhirr, curtly.

"Looks as if he had a tumble, though."

"I had to give him a push," explained the Captain.

Jukes gave an impatient sigh.

"It will come very sudden," said Captain MacWhirr, "and from over there, I fancy. God only knows, though. These books are only good to muddle your head and make you jumpy. It will be bad, and there's an end. If we only can steam her round in time to meet it . . ."

A minute passed. Some of the stars winked rapidly and vanished.

"You left them pretty safe?" began the Captain abruptly, as though the silence were unbearable.

"The coolies, sir? I rigged lifelines all ways across that tween-deck."

"Did you? Good idea, Mr. Jukes."

"I didn't . . . think you cared to . . . know," said Jukes—the lurching of the ship cut his speech—"how I got on with . . . that infernal job. We did it. And it may not matter in the end."

"Had to do what's fair, for all—they are Chinamen. Give them the same chance with ourselves—hang it all. She isn't lost yet. Bad enough to be shut up below in a gale—"

"That's what I thought when you gave me the job, sir," interjected Jukes, moodily.

"—without being battered to pieces," pursued Captain Mac-Whirr with rising vehemence. "Couldn't let that go on in my ship, if I knew she hadn't five minutes to live. Couldn't bear it, Mr. Jukes."

A hollow echoing noise, like that of a shout rolling in a rocky chasm, approached the ship and went away again. The last star, blurred, enlarged, as if returning to the fiery mist of its beginning, struggled with the colossal depth of blackness hanging over the ship—and went out.

"Now for it!" muttered Captain MacWhirr. "Mr. Jukes."

"Here, sir."

The two men were growing indistinct to each other.

"We must trust her to go through it and come out on the other side. That's plain and straight. There's no room for Captain Wilson's storm strategy here."

"No, sir."

"She will be smothered and swept again for hours," mumbled the Captain. "There's not much left by this time above deck for the sea to take away—unless you or me."

"Both, sir," whispered Jukes, breathlessly.

"You are always meeting trouble halfway, Jukes," Captain MacWhirr remonstrated quaintly. "Though it's a fact that the second mate is no good. D'ye hear, Mr. Jukes? You would be left alone if . . ."

Captain MacWhirr interrupted himself, and Jukes, glancing on all sides, remained silent.

"Don't you be put out by anything," the Captain continued, rather fast. "Keep her facing it. They may say what they like, but the heaviest seas run with the wind. Facing it—always facing it—that's the way to get through. You are a young sailor. Face it. That's enough for any man. Keep a cool head."

"Yes, sir," said Jukes, with a flutter of the heart.

In the next few seconds the Captain spoke to the engine room and got an answer.

For some reason Jukes experienced an access of confidence, a sensation that came from outside like a warm breath. It made him feel equal to every demand. The distant muttering of the darkness stole into his ears. He noted it unmoved, out of that sudden belief in himself, as a man safe in a shirt of mail would watch the point of a lance.

The ship labored without intermission amongst the black hills of water. She rumbled in her depths, shaking a white plummet of steam into the night, and Jukes' thought skimmed through the engine room, where Mr. Rout—good man—was ready. When the rumbling ceased it seemed to him that there was a pause of every sound, a dead pause in which Captain MacWhirr's voice rang out startlingly.

"What's that? A puff of wind?"—it spoke much louder than Jukes had ever heard it before—"On the bow. That's right. She may come out of it yet."

The mutter of the winds drew near. From far off could be distinguished the growth of a multiple clamor, marching and expanding. There was the throb as of many drums in it, and a vicious note like the chant of a tramping multitude.

Jukes could no longer see his captain distinctly. The darkness was piling itself upon the ship. At most he made out movements, a hint of elbows spread out, of a head thrown up.

Captain MacWhirr was trying to do up the top button of his oilskin coat. The hurricane, with its power to madden the seas, to sink ships, to uproot trees, to overturn strong walls and dash the very birds of the air to the ground, had found this taciturn man in its path, and, doing its utmost, had managed to wring a few words out of him.

Before the renewed wrath of winds swooped on his ship, Captain MacWhirr was moved to declare, in a tone of vexation, as it were, "I wouldn't like to lose her."

He was spared that annoyance.

CHAPTER VI

ON A BRIGHT SUNSHINY DAY, with the breeze chasing her smoke, the *Nan-Shan* came into Foochow. Her arrival was at once noticed on shore, and the seamen in the harbor said, "Look! Look at that steamer. Just look!"

She seemed, indeed, to have been used as a running target for the batteries of a cruiser. A hail of shells could not have given her upperworks a more broken, torn, and devastated aspect; and she had about her the worn, weary air of ships coming from the far ends of the world—and indeed with truth, for in her short passage she had been very far; sighting, verily, even the coast of the Great Beyond, whence no ship ever returns to give up her crew to the dust of the earth. She was encrusted and gray with salt to the top of her funnel, as though (as some facetious seaman said) "the crowd on board had fished her out from the bottom of the sea and brought her here for salvage." And further, excited by his own wit, he offered to give five pounds for her—"as she stands."

Before she had been quite an hour at rest, a meager little man, with a red-tipped nose and an angry face, landed from a sampan on the quay of the Foreign Concession, and incontinently turned to shake his fist at her.

A tall individual, with legs much too thin for a rotund stomach, and with watery eyes, strolled up and remarked, "Just left her— eh? Quick work."

He wore a soiled blue flannel suit with a pair of dirty cricketing shoes; a dingy gray mustache drooped from his lips, and daylight could be seen in two places between the rim and the crown of his hat.

"Hallo! What are you doing here?" asked the ex-second mate of the *Nan-Shan*, shaking hands hurriedly.

"Standing by for a job—got a quiet hint," explained the man in jerky, apathetic wheezes.

The second shook his fist again at the *Nan-Shan*. "There's a fellow there that ain't fit to have the command of a scow," he declared, quivering with passion, while the other looked about listlessly.

"Is there?"

But he caught sight on the quay of a heavy seaman's chest, lashed with new Manila line. He eyed it with awakened interest.

"I would talk and raise trouble if it wasn't for that damned Siamese flag. Nobody to go to—or I would make it hot for him. The fraud! You can't think . . ."

"Got your money all right?" inquired his seedy acquaintance.

"Yes. Paid me off on board," raged the second mate. "'Get your breakfast on shore,' says he."

"Mean skunk!" commented the tall man sympathetically. He passed his tongue on his lips. "Look! What about having a drink of some sort? Can't talk here. Let's get a fellow to carry your chest. I know a quiet place. . . ."

Mr. Jukes, who had been scanning the shore through a pair of glasses, informed the chief engineer afterwards that "our late second mate hasn't been long in finding a friend. A chap looking uncommonly like a bummer. I saw them walk away together."

The hammering and banging of the needful repairs did not disturb Captain MacWhirr. The steward found in the letter he wrote, in a tidy chart room, passages of such absorbing interest that twice he was nearly caught in the act.

But Mrs. MacWhirr, in the drawing room of the forty-pound house, stifled a yawn.

She was alone, reclining in a plush-bottomed gilt chair near a tiled fireplace, with Japanese fans on the mantel and a glow of coals in the grate. Lifting her hands, she glanced wearily here and there into the many pages. It was not her fault they were so prosy, so completely uninteresting—from "My darling wife" at the beginning to "Your loving husband" at the end. She couldn't be really expected to understand all these ship affairs. She was glad, of course, to hear from him, but she had never asked herself why, precisely.

". . . They are called typhoons. . . . The mate did not seem to like it. . . . Not in books. . . . Couldn't think of letting it go on. . . ."

The paper rustled sharply. ". . . A calm that lasted more than twenty minutes," she read perfunctorily; and the next words her thoughtless eyes caught, on top of another page, were: "see you and the children again . . ."

She made a movement of impatience. He was always thinking of coming home. He had never had such a good salary before. What was the matter now?

It did not occur to her to turn back overleaf to look. She would have found it recorded there that between 4 and 6 a.m. on December 25, Captain MacWhirr did actually think that his ship could not possibly live another hour in such a sea, and that he would never see his wife and children again. Nobody was to know this (his letters got mislaid so quickly)—nobody whatever but the steward, who had been greatly impressed by that disclosure. So much so, that he tried to give the cook some idea of the "narrow squeak we all had" by saying solemnly, "The old man himself had a dam' poor opinion of our chance."

"How do you know?" asked, contemptuously, the cook. "He hasn't told you, maybe?"

"Well, he did give me a hint to that effect," the steward brazened it out.

"Get along with you! He will be coming to tell *me* next," jeered the cook.

Mrs. MacWhirr glanced farther, on the alert. ". . . Do what's fair. . . . Miserable objects. . . . Only three, with a broken leg each, and one . . . hope to have done the fair thing. . . ."

She let fall her hands. No, there was nothing more about coming home. Must have been merely expressing a pious wish. Mrs. Mac-Whirr's mind was set at ease.

The door flew open, and a girl in the long-legged, short-frocked period of existence, flung into the room. A lot of colorless, rather lanky hair was scattered over her shoulders. Seeing her mother, she stood still, and directed her pale prying eyes upon the letter.

"From Father," murmured Mrs. MacWhirr. "What have you done with your ribbon?"

The girl put her hands up to her head and pouted.

"He's well," continued Mrs. MacWhirr, languidly. "At least I think so. He never says." She had a little laugh. The girl's face expressed a wandering indifference, and Mrs. MacWhirr surveyed her with fond pride.

"Go and get your hat," she said after a while. "I am going shopping. There is a sale at Linom's."

"Oh, how jolly!" uttered the child, impressively, in unexpectedly grave vibrating tones, and bounded out of the room.

It was a fine afternoon, with a gray sky and dry sidewalks. Outside the draper's Mrs. MacWhirr smiled upon a woman in a black mantle of generous proportions armored in jet and crowned with flowers. They broke into a swift little babble of greetings and exclamations. Mrs. MacWhirr talked rapidly.

"Thank you very much. He's not coming home yet. Of course it's very sad to have him away, but it's such a comfort to know he keeps so well. The climate there agrees with him," she added, beamingly, as if poor MacWhirr had been away touring in China for the sake of his health.

Neither was the chief engineer coming home yet. Mrs. Rout also had had a letter.

"Solomon says wonders will never cease," she cried joyously at the old lady in her armchair by the fire.

Mr. Rout's mother moved slightly, her withered hands lying in black half-mittens on her lap. The eyes of the engineer's wife fairly danced on the paper.

"That captain of the ship he is in—a rather simple man, you remember, Mother?—has done something rather clever, Solomon says."

"Yes, my dear," said the old woman meekly, sitting with bowed silvery head. "I think I remember."

Solomon Rout, Old Sol, Father Sol, the Chief—Mr. Rout had been the baby of her many children—all dead by this time. And she remembered him best as a boy of ten. She had seen so little of him since, she had gone through so many years, that sometimes it seemed that her daughter-in-law was talking of some strange man.

Mrs. Rout junior was disappointed. "H'm. H'm." She turned the page. "How provoking! He doesn't say what it is. Says I couldn't understand how much there was in it. Fancy! What could it be so very clever? What a wretched man not to tell us!"

She read on without further remark soberly, and at last sat looking into the fire. The chief wrote just a word or two of the typhoon; but something had moved him to express an increased longing for the companionship of the jolly woman. "If it hadn't been that Mother must be looked after, I would send you your passage money today. You could set up a small house out here. I would have a chance to see you sometimes then. We are not growing younger. . . ."

"He's well, Mother," sighed Mrs. Rout, rousing herself.

"He always was a strong healthy boy," said the old woman.

But Mr. Jukes' account, written to his friend in the Western ocean trade, was really animated and very full. His friend imparted it freely to the other officers of his liner. "A chap I know writes to me about an extraordinary affair that happened on board his ship in a typhoon. It's the funniest thing! Just see for yourself what he says. I'll show you his letter."

There were phrases in it calculated to give the impression of lighthearted, indomitable resolution. Jukes had written them in good faith, for he felt thus when he wrote. He described with lurid effect the scenes in the tween-deck.

" . . . It struck me in a flash that those confounded Chinamen thought we were robbing them. 'Tisn't good to part the Chinaman from his money if he is the stronger party. We need have been desperate indeed to go thieving in such weather, but what could these beggars know of us? So, without thinking twice, I got the hands away in a jiffy. Our work was done—and we cleared out without staying to inquire how they felt. I am convinced that if they had not been so unmercifully shaken—and afraid to stand up—we would have been torn to pieces. Oh! It was something, I can tell you; and you may run to and fro across that old Atlantic to the end of time before you find yourself with such a job on your hands."

After this he alluded professionally to the damage done to the ship, and went on thus:

"It was when the weather quieted down that the situation became confoundedly delicate. It wasn't made any better by us having been lately transferred to the Siamese flag; though the skipper can't see that it makes any difference—'as long as *we* are on board'— he says. There are feelings that this man simply hasn't got—and there's an end of it. You might just as well try to make a bedpost understand. But apart from this it is an infernally lonely state for a ship to be going about the China seas with no proper consuls, not even a gunboat of her own anywhere, nor a body to go to in case of trouble.

"My notion was to keep these Johnnies under hatches for another fifteen hours or so, as we weren't much farther than that from Foochow. We would find there, most likely, some sort of a man-of-war, and once under her guns we were safe enough; for surely any skipper of a man-of-war—English, French, or Dutch—would see white men through as far as a row on board goes. We could get rid of the coolies and their money afterwards by delivering them to their mandarin or taotai, or whatever they call these chaps you see being carried about their streets in sedan chairs.

"But the old man wouldn't see it somehow. He wanted to keep the matter quiet. He got that notion into his head, and a steam windlass couldn't drag it out of him. He wanted as little fuss made as possible, for the sake of the ship's name and for the sake of the owners. It made me angry hot. By then, I'll admit, I could hardly keep on my feet. None of us had had a spell of any sort for nearly thirty hours, and there the old man sat rubbing his chin, rubbing the top of his head, and so bothered he hadn't even thought to pull his long boots off.

"'I hope, sir,' says I, 'you won't be letting them out on deck before we make ready for them in some shape or other.' Not, mind you, that I felt very sanguine about controlling these beggars if they meant to take charge. 'I wish,' said I, 'you would let us throw the whole lot of these dollars down to them and leave them to fight it out amongst themselves, while we get a rest.'

"'Now you talk wild, Jukes,' says he, looking up in his slow way. 'We must plan out something that would be fair to all parties.'

"I had no end of work on hand, as you may imagine, so I set the hands going, and then I thought I would turn in a bit. I hadn't been asleep in my bunk ten minutes when in rushes the steward.

"'For God's sake, Mr. Jukes, come out! Come on deck quick, sir. The Captain's letting them out. Oh, sir, save us! The chief engineer has just run below for his revolver.'

"That's what I understood the fool to say. However, Father Rout swears he had only gone to get a clean handkerchief. Anyhow, I made one jump into my trousers and flew on deck. There was certainly a good deal of noise going on forward of the bridge. Four of the hands with the boss'n were at work abaft. I passed up to them some of the rifles all the ships on the China coast carry in the cabin, and led them on the bridge.

"On the way I ran against Old Sol, looking startled.

"'Come along,' I shouted to him.

"We charged, the seven of us, up to the chart room. All was over. There stood the old man with his seaboots still drawn up to the hips and in shirt sleeves—got warm thinking it out, I suppose. Bun Hin's dandy clerk was at his elbow, still green in the face. I could see directly I was in for something.

"'What the devil are these monkey tricks, Mr. Jukes?' asks the old man, as angry as ever he could be. I tell you frankly it made me lose my tongue. 'For God's sake, Mr. Jukes,' says he, 'take these rifles away from the men. Somebody's sure to get hurt if you don't. Damme, this ship is worse than Bedlam! Look sharp now. I want you up here to help me and Bun Hin's Chinaman to count that money. You wouldn't mind lending a hand, too, Mr. Rout, now you are here. The more of us the better.'

"He had settled it all in his mind while I was having a snooze. Had we been an English ship, or only going to land our cargo of coolies in an English port, like Hong Kong, for instance, there would have been no end of inquiries, claims for damages, and so on. But these Chinamen know their officials better than we do.

"The hatches had been taken off already, and they were all on deck after a night and a day down below. It made you feel queer to see so many gaunt, wild faces together. The beggars stared about at the sky, at the sea, at the ship, as though they had expected the whole thing to have been blown to pieces. And no wonder! They had had a doing that would have shaken the soul out of any man. But then they say a Chinaman has no soul. He has, though, something about him that is deuced tough. There was a fellow (amongst others of the badly hurt) who had had his eye all but knocked out. It stood out of his head the size of half a hen's egg. This would have laid out a white man on his back for a month, and yet there was that chap elbowing here and there in the crowd and talking to the others as if nothing had been the matter. They made a great hubbub amongst themselves, and whenever the old man showed his bald head on the foreside of the bridge, they would all leave off jawing and look at him from below.

"It seems that after he had done his thinking he made that Bun Hin's fellow go down and explain to them the only way they could get their money back. He told me afterwards that, all the coolies having worked in the same place and for the same length of time, he reckoned he would be doing the fair thing by them as near as possible if he shared all the cash we had picked up equally among the lot. You couldn't tell one man's dollars from another's, he said, and if you asked each man how much money he brought on board he was afraid they would lie, and he would find himself a long way short. I think he was right there. As to giving up the money to any Chinese official he could scare up in Foochow, he said he might just as well put the lot in his own pocket at once for all the good it would be to them. I suppose they thought so, too.

"We finished the distribution before dark. It was rather a sight: the sea running high, the ship a wreck to look at, these Chinamen staggering up on the bridge one by one for their share, and the old man still booted and in his shirt sleeves, busy paying out at the chart-room door, perspiring like anything, and now and then coming down sharp on myself or Father Rout about one thing or another not quite to his mind. He himself took the share of those who were disabled to them on the Number Two hatch. There were three dollars left over, and these went to the three most damaged coolies, one to each. We turned to afterwards, and shoveled out on deck heaps of wet rags, all sorts of fragments of things without shape, and that you couldn't give a name to, and let them settle the ownership themselves.

"This certainly is coming as near as can be to keeping the thing quiet for the benefit of all concerned. What's your opinion, you pampered mail-boat swell? The old chief says that this was plainly the only thing that could be done. The skipper remarked to me the other day, 'There are things you find nothing about in books.' I think that he got out of it very well for such a stupid man."

Joseph Conrad
(1857–1924)

IN THE SPRING of 1893, the clipper ship *Torrens* was making her way across the Pacific, bound home to England from Australia. One of her passengers, an aspiring writer named John Galsworthy, wrote a letter to a friend describing one of the ship's officers:

> The first mate is a Pole called Conrad. . . . He is a man of travel and experience in many parts of the world, and has a fund of yarns on which I draw freely. He has been right up in the Congo and all around Malacca and Borneo . . . to say nothing of a little smuggling in the days of his youth.

The well-traveled sailor Galsworthy was describing was Joseph Conrad.

Joseph Conrad was born Jozef Teodor Konrad Korzeniowski on December 3, 1857. His father was a member of a revolutionary group seeking to free Poland from Russian domination. In 1861 Conrad's father was arrested and sent to northern Russia. His wife and son followed him into exile. Two years later Conrad's mother died. In 1867 Conrad and his father were allowed to return to Poland. Soon after, his father died and Conrad went to live with his Uncle Tadeusz. Conrad read widely and had a natural curiosity but did poorly in school. In 1874 he asked his uncle for permission to join the French merchant marine.

In April 1878 Conrad signed aboard a British freighter, and he sailed aboard British ships for the next sixteen years. His voyages took him around the world, from Australia to Singapore. In 1884 he was naturalized as a British citizen. In that same year he was awarded his master's certificate, which qualified him to command ships. Jozef Korzeniowski became Joseph Conrad, British Master Mariner.

In 1889 Conrad obtained command of a river steamer in the Congo, a Belgian colony in Africa. He spent four terrible months there before illness forced him to leave, but that brief time provided him with the raw material for one of his greatest works, the short novel *The Heart of Darkness*.

In January 1894 Conrad moved to London when a planned voyage to Canada fell through. His life as a rover and man of action was over, and his career as a writer was about to begin.

Five years earlier Conrad had started a novel set in the East Indies. While living in London, waiting for a ship to command, Conrad finished the book. At the urging of friends, he submitted the manuscript to a publisher. To his surprise and relief, *Almayer's Folly* was published in 1895 and received favorable critical attention.

Novels and short stories followed in quick succession. Two novels, *Lord Jim* and *Nostromo*, and the short novels *Youth*, *The Heart of Darkness*, and *The Secret Sharer* made his reputation as a master storyteller and observer of the human condition. In 1903 Conrad published *Typhoon and Other Stories*. *Typhoon*, one of Conrad's most popular works, was based on a disastrous voyage he had made in 1887.

In March 1896 Conrad married Jessie George, a secretary fifteen years his junior. The good-natured Jessie complemented Conrad's often nervous temperament. The couple had two sons.

Conrad was a moody man, given to periods of depression. The romanticism of his youth gave way to pessimism in his later years. His health, broken by his time in the Congo, declined as he grew old. On August 3, 1924, he died, a month after turning down the British government's offer of a knighthood.

Other Titles by Joseph Conrad

The Heart of Darkness and the Secret Sharer. New York: New American Library, 1971.

Lord Jim. New York: Bantam, 1981.

Nostromo. New York: Penguin, 1984.

The Portable Conrad. Revised edition. Morton D. Zabel and Frederick R. Carl, editors. New York: Viking, 1976.

The Secret Agent. New York: Bantam, 1984.

Typhoon and Other Stories. Cedric Watts, editor. New York: Oxford University Press, 1986.

Youth and the End of the Tether. New York: Penguin, 1976.